GET MORE OF MY BOOKS FREE!

To say thank you for buying this book, I'd like to invite you to my exclusive *VIP Club*, and give you some of my books and short stories for FREE.

To join the club, head to adamcroft.net/vip-club **and two free books will be sent to you straight away! And the best thing is it won't cost you a penny — ever.**

Click here to join the VIP Club

Adam Croft

For more information, visit my website: adamcroft.net

Just like my food, money and receding hairline, this book is for James.

1

Saturday morning is my favourite time of the week. No kids, no work, no stress. It's the only chance I get to actually be myself.

I don't need to be Supermum at home or Amy'll-Do-It at work. I get to do what I want to do, in my own time, for five whole hours.

Harry and Jacob being two years apart means they are — for the time being — in different age groups when it comes to football. Harry plays in the under-10s, and Jacob for the under-8s. The beauty of that is that the under-10s play at nine o'clock in the morning, and the under-8s don't kick off until midday.

Brendan's great. He takes the pair of them every Saturday morning, and Jacob waits patiently while Harry plays his match, then they head to a nearby café for brunch before going back for Jacob's game.

The house is eerily quiet on Saturday mornings, but that's the way I like it. The only sound I want to hear is my own breathing.

If the weather's good, as it is at this time of year, I like to sit out in the garden with a book.

The garden's not a conventional shape (Brendan called it 'weird' when we first viewed the house, and still swears he got ten grand off the asking price for it). It curves and sort of doglegs at the end, leaving a nice secluded decking area, a perfect morning suntrap for a mug of coffee and a few chapters. No view of any build-ings or people. Just me in my own little oasis.

During the winter, or whenever the weather's colder, I'll quite often take a bath. The enforced solitude — even though the house is empty — is so relaxing.

Saturday mornings are about the only time I get to read. I always try and get another chapter down before going to sleep, but I'll inevitably fall asleep with the book on my face after about three paragraphs.

Even holidays aren't as relaxing as they were before we had the boys. We were in Tenerife only a couple of weeks ago, but I swear Brendan and I came home more stressed than before we left.

The idea of being able to lay on a beach and do nothing just isn't realistic when you're trying to stop two kids from fighting or destroying each other's belongings. Brendan said it was 'cabin fever'. I told him I've got no idea how you can get cabin fever while you're sitting on miles of open beach, staring across the vast ocean at the coast of Africa.

But then again the boys have never been ones for playing together. We thought having them only two years apart would mean they'd grow up together, but other than football they don't really share many interests.

Harry's very much into his computer games. He'd spend all day playing online if we let him. He's loud, energetic and very much in charge. Jacob, on the other hand, is more like me. He's easy going. He much prefers to sit in peace with a book. We stick together, me and Jacob.

It's due to be a blisteringly hot day. It's already unbearably warm and muggy, and the parasol is doing little to keep the heat away. The sun might be kept at bay, but the air is still and there's no hiding from the humidity.

I decide to get up and go inside for a glass of iced water. The house will be even hotter than it is out here — one of the downsides to living in an old building — but the thought of an ice cold drink is too much to resist right now.

As I open the fridge, I hear banging on my front door and window. Furrowing my brow, I walk through the house to the front door, and open it.

Two uniformed police officers are standing on my front doorstep.

'Good morning. We're looking for a Mrs Amy Walker,' one of them says, looking beyond me and into the house, as the other casts his eye over me.

'Uh, yes. That's me,' I say. 'What's happened?'

The other officer nods. 'Amy Walker, I'm arresting you on suspicion of murder. You do not have to say anything. But, it may harm your defence if you do not mention when questioned something which you later rely on in court. Anything you do say may be given in evidence.'

2

'No, please,' I say, as my eyes scan the scene outside. 'Not handcuffs. I'm not going anywhere.'

There's a marked police car parked on the driveway, and the first thought to cross my mind is that I didn't give them permission to park there.

'Mrs Walker, do you understand what I just said to you?'

I blink a few times, trying to take it all in. 'Uh, yes. No. You're arresting me, but I don't know what for.'

'You're being arrested on suspicion of the murder of Roger Walker,' one of the officers says. Their voices are beginning to blend into one. I can't tell which one's which.

'Roger?' I whisper, my throat dry and my voice hoarse. 'How can I have murdered him?'

'It'll all be gone through in an interview at the police

station, Mrs Walker. Until then it's best you don't say anything more.'

I feel the handcuffs snap around my wrists. I didn't even notice they were still trying to put them on me. I feel a small tug as I'm pulled towards the waiting police car.

'I need to lock the door,' I say.

'Is there anyone else in the house?'

'No. No, just me.'

'Where's the key?'

'Inside the door. In the lock.'

My brain's fighting between trying to make sense of what the police just told me, what's now happening and somehow trying to focus on the mundane activity of getting my front door locked.

'This is all some huge mistake,' I say. 'Roger's not dead. He can't be.'

'Mrs Walker, I really must advise you to save it for the interview. You're going to give us a hell of a lot of paper-work otherwise.'

My whole body feels numb as someone puts their hand on top of my head and guides me into the back of the police car. The door closes silently, the only sound being the pounding of the blood in my ears.

And that's when it begins to sink in. Not fully, not properly, but the first grains of realisation hit me like an avalanche.

I'm under arrest for the murder of my father-in-law.

3

The car comes to a stop in the gated car park of the police station. It goes quiet for a moment, before my door opens and a hand reaches in to help me out.

I'm taken through into an area which I can only describe as bleak. The stifling summer atmosphere aside, everything about it feels cold. There's a deep musty smell, pierced with the sharp tang of disinfectant.

'Good morning, gentlemen. Who do we have here?' the man behind the desk says. I open my mouth to answer, but one of the police officers gets there first.

'This is Mrs Amy Walker.'

'Amy Walker. And the charge?'

'Sus murder. I was sent to Mrs Walker's home address to arrest her following an incident at an address in Missingham Drive earlier this morning, in which a man died.'

'Sus murder,' the man says, as if suspected murder is

the most normal thing in the world, as he types into his computer. 'Okay, Amy. Have you been arrested before?'

I shake my head. 'No. Of course not.'

'Okay. Do you understand why you've been arrested?'

'Uh, sort of.' I know what they're saying, but it doesn't make any sense. 'I didn't do anything to anyone. I haven't been anywhere near Roger's house. I've been at home all morning.' My head is pounding.

'Okay, we can save all that for the formal interview. For now I just need to make sure you understand that you've been arrested on suspicion of murder.' He looks at me, waiting for me to answer.

'Yes. I think so.'

'Alright.' He points to a laminated sheet of paper on the wall. 'This notice here tells you all about your rights. You're entitled to regular breaks for food and to use the toilet. I presume you don't require the services of a translator. Do you have any health conditions we should be aware of?'

I shake my head.

'And how are you feeling at the moment?'

'Confused.'

'Confused,' he says, typing it into the computer. 'You're entitled to free legal advice if you want it. Do you have a solicitor?'

'Uh, yes. No. I don't know. I'd... I'd call Roger and ask him to sort something out.'

'Roger being...?'

'My father in law.'

'The victim,' one of the other officers clarifies.

'Ah. Well, in that case I think we can safely say that's not practical. Would you like us to arrange for you to see the duty solicitor?'

It feels like a thousand drills are boring through my skull. 'Uh, I don't know. Do I need one? I haven't done anything.'

'Well, it's your decision to make, but you have just been arrested on suspicion of murder. If it was me, I think I'd probably want some legal advice.'

I nod. 'Okay.'

'Now, is there anyone you want us to call to let them know where you are? Your next of kin? A friend, perhaps?'

I haven't even thought about this. Brendan and the boys will be home in a couple of hours. How on earth am I meant to explain this to them? I can only hope that it's all sorted out before then. Surely they've got to realise pretty quickly there's been some sort of mistake.

'I don't know. My husband.'

One of the officers who arrested me speaks to the man behind the desk. 'We'd need to tread carefully there. Mr Walker is the son of the deceased. We've not been able to track him down yet, and that probably isn't going to be the best way for him to find out.'

'Quite. Is there a friend we can call, Amy?'

'No. Just Brendan.'

'Do you know where he is?' one of the arresting officers asks me.

'Yeah. At the football pitches on the other side of the village. Harry and Jacob, our sons, play football every Saturday morning. He'll be there with them until lunchtime.'

'Do you have a photo of him?'

'Uh. Yeah. There'll be some on my phone. Why?'

'We'll need to go and speak to him. He probably won't be aware of any of this yet.'

'But you can't tell him. You can't tell him his dad's dead. He's not. He can't be. You'll upset him. And then when you realise you're wrong it'll… Just don't!'

'Mrs Walker, if you want us to call someone else to let them know where you are, we can, but either way we have to inform Mr Walker that his father has died. He's Roger's next of kin since your mother-in-law died, yes?'

'Well yes, but… How did you know that? How do you know Belinda's dead?'

'Where is your phone, Amy?' the man behind the desk asks.

I rub my temples. 'Uh, I lost it.'

'You lost it?'

'Yeah.'

'So you don't have a mobile phone?'

'I do, but I lost it. I don't know where it is.'

The police officers share a look. 'I presume there are

photos of your husband in your house?' one of the arresting officers asks.

'Yeah. Of course. Look, can someone please tell me what's going on? This is insane!'

'All in good time,' the man behind the desk says. 'You'll get the chance to ask questions and answer them in your interview. We'll pop her in F3, chaps.'

There's an arm on my shoulder before I realise what's happening. I can barely breathe, but I try to force the words out.

'Wait. I need to speak to someone. What's going on? What's happened? Why are you doing this to me?'

The police officer ignores my questions and guides me into a bright room.

4

'Okay Amy, we're going to need to take your clothes from you now. Can you take off what you're wearing, please, and put these on.' The female officer gestures to what looks like a pair of grey jogging bottoms and matching t-shirt. 'There's a rather fetching jumper to complete the set, but I thought it might be a bit warm for that,' she says, smiling. I don't see what there is to smile about.

'When will I get them back?' I ask. They're not items I'm particularly attached to, but it would be nice to know when I'm going to see them again.

'Impossible to say, I'm afraid. They'll be checked for any forensic evidence, so it depends what they find.'

I look at her for a moment, then realise I have no option. I take my clothes off and watch as she puts each item of clothing into individual bags. She even bags each shoe and sock separately. It's both impressive and incredibly scary how meticulous and organised the whole operation is.

Once she's finished sealing each bag and labelling them, she hands them over to another police officer.

'Right, if you follow me through here,' she says, opening the door, 'we just need to finish booking you in.'

I walk through the door and across the corridor, into the room she indicated.

'Now we're going to take your fingerprints and a sample of your DNA, as well as some photos, alright?'

I nod. It doesn't sound like I have much choice.

'What… what is it used for?' I ask.

'The fingerprints and DNA? For our records, and to cross-reference with any fingerprints or DNA found at the scene of the crime.'

'But it's my father-in-law's house,' I say. 'We're there every week.'

'Don't worry, I'm sure the investigation will take all that into account.' She guides me over to a machine that looks like an old office photocopier. 'If you just place your thumbs in these little squares here,' she says, manoeuvring my hands into place. 'That's great. Okay, hold it there for a moment.' She repeats the process for my other fingers. I wonder how long it's been since they stopped using ink pads.

'Okay, now can you stand just behind that white line on the floor, please, facing me.'

Before I realise what she's doing, the camera clicks three times.

'Now turn to face that wall over there, please.'

Another three clicks.

'And spin round to face this wall over here, please.'

Click. Click. Click.

'Okay, that's great. Now I'm going to take a couple of samples of DNA from you. That'll be in the form of a swab from the inside of your mouth. It's very quick and totally painless. Do I have your consent for that?'

I stumble and stammer for a minute. I didn't even realise this was a *thing*.

'Do I have any choice?' I say.

She smiles. 'Yes and no. You can decline, but then I'd have to get the authorisation of an Inspector, at which point reasonable force can be used to obtain the samples, so it's probably easier this way.'

I swallow. 'Alright.'

I can't explain how dehumanising and degrading it feels to be in this anonymous room, in someone else's clothes, having my whole identity reduced to a double helix; a chemical strand which could determine my whole future.

I open my mouth when she tells me to, and she scrapes the cotton bud around the inside of both cheeks, before popping it into a sealed container.

'Okay, that's it. I just need to take some fingernail scrapings from you now,' she says.

'Why?'

'It's been requested by the on-call SIO.' She registers my blank look. 'Senior Investigating Officer. The detective in charge of the investigation.'

Detective. Jesus Christ. In the space of less than ninety minutes I've gone from sitting in my garden with a good book to having my fingernail scrapings requested by a murder detective. My brain can't even begin to comprehend what's going on.

'Uh, okay. Fine,' I say.

She gives me that smile again — the one that's meant to disarm and reassure me, but which actually just gives me the creeps.

Once she's done, she bags everything up, hands it over to another officer and leads me to my cell.

5

I've cried myself into exhaustion. I don't think I was asleep — just catatonic.

The sound of my cell door opening jolts me back into the present, and I sit up on the blue mattress that is my bed, my sweaty skin slipping against the plastic as I try to move myself.

'Amy, your solicitor's here to see you,' the police officer says.

I immediately thank my lucky stars that Roger has sent someone to help me. It's exactly the sort of thing he'd do. He's a true family man, and he's always got everyone's back. It's a couple of seconds before I arrive back in reality and register that this is the duty solicitor the police said they'd arrange for me.

Because Roger is dead.

And they think I killed him.

'Follow me,' the officer says.

I stand, or at least try to. My legs feel like jelly. Eventually, I manage to put one foot in front of the other and I follow him out of the cell.

My stomach is churning, and I feel like I'm going to be sick. My whole body is a whirlwind of confusion, and I really don't see how I'm going to be able to hold on to any of this. Everything has been turned upside down and I can't see any way out.

I'm led into a small side room with a desk and two chairs. It's barely the size of a broom cupboard. A man in a suit comes in a few seconds later with a leather case under his arm.

'You must be Amy. I'm Brian Conway,' he says. 'I'm the duty solicitor today. How are you?'

'Uh, I don't know. Confused. Upset. I feel sick.'

'Okay. Well, you just give me a shout if you want to stop at any time, alright?'

I nod.

'Right. So, you've been arrested on suspicion of the murder of your father-in-law, Roger Walker. Is that right?'

I nod. 'I think so.'

'Okay. And what happened?'

I look at him. 'When?'

'Roger's death. Talk me through it. Were you at the scene?'

'No! The first I heard of it was when the police

knocked at my door and arrested me. I didn't even know he was dead.'

'Alright. So do you have any idea why the police arrested you? As I understand it, he was only killed this morning. It's very strange for the police to immediately turn up and arrest you without having good reason to think you were there. Did you go out at all this morning?'

'No. I've been at home since I got home from work last night. I was sitting out in my garden reading a book, and I came inside and heard a knock on the door and… And that was it. They were there.'

'Is there anyone at home who could verify that?'

I rub my forehead. 'Brendan, my husband, and our boys were at home with me all night. They went to football early this morning.'

'And you've been on your own since?'

'Yeah.'

'At home?'

'Yeah.'

'Okay. Well the lack of an alibi isn't massively helpful, but the onus is on them to prove that you were at the scene, not on us to prove you weren't. So if you weren't, then presumably there's no way they can prove it and no way it'll go to a charge.'

I look at him. 'Presumably?'

'Well, if what you're telling me is correct, I mean.'

'And why wouldn't it be?'

'It's a very serious charge, Mrs Walker. I don't expect

anyone to sit down with me and tell me they did it. But I'm working for you, and if you tell me you were at home all morning and the first you heard of your father-in-law's death was when the police turned up at your door, I will take your word for that. It's up to the police to prove otherwise. A large part of my job is making sure they do theirs properly, and ensuring justice is done. Now, the next stage is going to be a formal interview. That'll be with Detective Inspector McKenna. She's tough. She'll try to crack you. This is the first time you'll hear their reasons for suspecting you, and it's the first opportunity I'll get to examine any evidence or reasoning they have. At this stage I'd advise you to answer "no comment" to all of their questions.'

'Why?' I ask. 'Doesn't that just make me sound guilty?'

'Not if you're not. Like I said, it's their job to prove it — not ours to disprove it. If there's nothing they can prove, you don't want to go down the line of incriminating yourself by saying something you shouldn't. You have the right to say nothing, and in this situation I'd strongly advise that's what you do. Understood?'

I look down at the table and nod.

6

SATURDAY 4 AUGUST, 12.55PM.

The interview room is exactly how it looks on TV. A small-ish space, with one door, one table and four chairs around it. Brian and I sit on one side of the table, and two plain-clothes police officers — a man and a woman — sit on the other.

'Ready?' the female officer asks. I say nothing, but Brian nods gently on my behalf. She presses a button on the recording equipment on the table, and it emits a loud, long beep.

'Interview with Amy Walker, in the presence of myself, Detective Inspector Jane McKenna, Detective Constable Mark Brennan and Amy's solicitor, Brian Conway. Amy, you've been arrested and detained on suspicion of the murder of Roger Walker. Can you explain your relationship to him please?'

I look at Brian. Surely he doesn't want me to no-comment this question, too? He gives me a nod to indicate that I should go ahead, but that doesn't tell me whether he wants me to go ahead and answer the question or go ahead as planned. I decide not to take any risks.

'No comment.'

McKenna flashes a look at Brian.

'Alright. We understand he's your father-in-law. Do you have any objections to us making that assumption?'

'No comment.'

'The arresting officers said you expressed some surprise when you found out that Roger had died. Can you tell us about that?

'No comment.'

'When did you last see your father-in-law, Amy?'

'No comment.'

'Where were you this morning?'

'No comment.'

'Were you at his house?'

'No comment.'

'Did you kill Roger, Amy?'

My throat catches as they hit me with the direct question, and I can feel my eyes fluttering. The accusation is like a sucker punch to the gut.

'No comment,' I say, my voice weak.

'Do you know how he died?'

I don't. But I want to. I think. 'No comment.'

'He was attacked with a blunt instrument while he sat

at his kitchen table. We don't know what was used yet, but there wasn't a whole lot left of his skull. There are some defensive wounds, but not many. He was probably dead within seconds. It looks to me as if he was sitting at his kitchen table, enjoying a nice cup of tea, perhaps having a chat with someone he knew, when this attack came out of the blue. Who do you know who'd do that, Amy?'

I try to hold back the bile in my throat. Just hearing how Roger died is making me feel sick. 'No comment.'

'I mean, presumably it was someone he knew. There's no sign of forced entry, for example. And if a complete stranger or unexpected visitor walked into his kitchen while he was sitting at the table you might reasonably assume he'd stand up, no? Perhaps confront the person. But he didn't. That tells me he knew his killer. Let them into his house. Welcomed them inside. A friend, perhaps. Or a family member.'

McKenna lets this hang in the air. She hasn't asked me a question, so I don't speak.

'Do you know a man by the name of Eric Black?'

I look at McKenna. 'No. No… no comment.'

'No? He's your father-in-law's next-door neighbour. Have you met him before?'

I think for a moment. I don't think I have, but I imagine I've probably seen him in his front garden at some point when we've turned up at the house. I doubt I could pick him out of an identity parade.

'No comment.'

'Only he seems to know you. He recognised you earlier today. He says he saw you coming out of your father-in-law's house following what sounded like an altercation. He said you seemed "harried and distressed",' McKenna says, reading from her notes. 'Why were you harried and distressed, Amy?'

My heart is racing and I can feel my whole world closing in on me. None of this makes any sense. None of it. I've never even heard of Eric Black. I haven't been to Roger's house in days. Probably a week. I wasn't there earlier today; I was in my garden, reading a book. Why would anyone say otherwise?

I can prove it. I must be able to prove it. Brian told me I don't need to. He told me it's up to the police to prove I was there. I know that. And I know they can't prove I was there, because I wasn't. But that still doesn't stop the feeling of complete and utter dread, of absolute injustice.

Why would Roger's neighbour say that? Maybe he's insane. Perhaps he's delusional. Eric. He sounds old. Maybe his eyesight's going. Alzheimer's, perhaps. That can be proven, if so. I'm sure they can do a test on him, and when it gets to court they'd…

Oh god. Court. Just the thought of the word sends a bolt of ice down my spine. It won't get that far. It can't. They'll soon realise it's all a dreadful misunderstanding and I'll be let out, allowed back home to my kids and my husband. My husband whose father is dead and who will forever have the nagging doubt, the slightest lingering suspicion that maybe I did it.

'Amy? Why were you harried and distressed?'

I look at Brian. He flicks his eyebrows at me, another imperceptible piece of code which I now assume only solicitors and hardened criminals are meant to decode.

'No comment.'

'Amy, I know your solicitor will have briefed you to no-comment your way through this interview, but I do have a duty to inform you that, if this goes to court, a jury won't look too kindly on you not cooperating with the investigation. Judges have been known to give harsher sentences in these situations, too.'

Brian interjects. 'Detective Inspector, you know full well that my client has the right to answer in any way she wishes. If she wants to let you know that she has no comment, that is her prerogative. Any mentions of court cases are completely unfair and misguided, too. You've not yet displayed any evidence which would result in a recommendation to charge, so you're not within a million miles of a court case. Please don't try to intimidate my client in this way.'

'I'm not trying to intimidate anyone, Mr Conway. I'm letting Amy know — as is my duty under the Police and Criminal Evidence Act — that anything she says or doesn't say in a formal interview situation will have an impact on any future trial.'

'Nonsense. You know she's never been in trouble with

the police before, and you're throwing insinuations of trials, judges and juries around as if they're a foregone conclusion. Now, if you could please return to the matter in hand.'

McKenna looks at him for a few moments, then smiles.

'Certainly. Amy, do you own a mobile phone?'

'Yes,' I say, without even thinking. I look at Brian. He purses his lips. I look away. I don't see any way in which I can incriminate myself by admitting I own a mobile phone. Who doesn't? They can check that sort of stuff anyway. And above all else, I just want to get out of here. I know Brian said it's up to them to prove it, but the sooner I can prove I had nothing to do with it, the sooner we can end this whole mess.

'What sort of phone is it?'

Again, all stuff they can check. 'An iPhone 7 Plus.'

'Is that the big one?'

I nod.

'Out loud, please, Amy.'

'Yes,' I say. Brian doesn't know the background, doesn't know for sure I'm innocent. He's playing it safe. I get that. But I didn't do anything, and the sooner I cooperate with the police, the sooner they can discover I'm innocent and I can go home. Saying *no comment* to everything is only going to make me look guilty. I've got nothing to hide.

'Where is it? It wasn't bagged with your belongings when you were brought in.'

I swallow. 'Uh, I lost it.'

'You lost it? Where?'

'I don't know. Sometimes I forget and leave it places. At work, usually.'

'Would you say you're a careless and disorganised person, Amy?'

Brian puts his hand on my arm and looks at me, shaking his head slightly. He's indicating that I shouldn't answer, shouldn't be drawn into this.

'No. Not especially.'

'But you regularly forget or lose a smartphone worth a few hundred pounds?'

'I don't use it much. I don't do social media or anything like that. And the signal at home is crap anyway.'

'So you don't know where your mobile phone is at the moment?'

I blink a few times, then shake my head. 'No. No, I don't.'

McKenna smiles and nods. 'I see. Well, I think that'll be all for now.'

7

He took the key from his pocket and felt the cold steel against his fingers, the sharp ridges and notches now as familiar as an old friend. When he ran his finger across it, it reminded him of the ridges on an old music box. Except this one played the sweet song of revenge.

He slid the key into the door and held it firmly as he turned it slowly, letting his hand absorb the clicking of the latches. After three turns, the door was unlocked.

He pulled down gently on the door handle and let himself inside, keeping the door handle pulled down as he pushed the door gently to, before slowly lifting the handle back up.

He was inside.

He made his way across the carpet towards the kitchen, feeling for any creaky floorboards.

There weren't any.

He tried to keep his mind on the job in hand, but couldn't avoid sneaking a few glances at the photographs that adorned the walls and cabinets. This was clearly a happy family home.

For now.

Once in the kitchen, he headed straight for the two mobile phones sitting on the work surface, plugged in to charge for the night. They were exactly where he'd expected them to be.

He pressed a button on each of them to bring them to life.

One had a photo of two young boys playing football. The other had a picture of Brendan and the two boys.

Just to make doubly sure, he swiped his finger across the screen on the second phone to unlock it.

The screen asked him for four-digit security code. Without even assuming any other possibility, he entered her year of birth and watched as the screen unlocked. Her stupidity and naivety was causing her more problems than she knew.

He opened the phone's contact list and scrolled down. There was an entry for Brendan, but nothing under Amy. This must be hers.

He unplugged the phone, careful not to touch the charging lead with anything other than the sleeve of his jacket. Using a knuckle, he switched the lead off at the mains, then pocketed the phone.

He wiped his jacket sleeve across the front of Brendan's phone a few times, careful not to leave any fingerprints, then released a small accomplished sigh.

He retraced his steps back through the kitchen and hallway to the front door, before gently pulling down the handle once again. Once the door was open, he used his jacket sleeve to wipe the inside handle clean, then closed the door silently.

He pulled the handle up, again allowing his hand to absorb the clicking of the latches as they slid into place, then he inserted the key and slowly turned it three times before wiping the outside of the handle with his sleeve.

He walked back down the front path, skirting close to the shrubs which lined the front garden. He swiped up on the phone's screen, then tapped the moon symbol to put it onto *Do Not Disturb* mode. That way, it would stay on but wouldn't ring or vibrate. He flicked the little switch on the side to silent mode, just in case.

At the end of the front path, he stood next to the raised bed and made sure he wasn't being watched. It was unlikely — he wasn't in view of any houses — but he couldn't afford to be too sure. One slip-up now and the whole game would be over. He couldn't risk that. There was far too much to lose.

Once he was sure the coast was clear, he reached into the conifers and deposited the phone, covering it over with a mulch of leaves and dropped needles, barely breaking his stride as he did so.

He smiled inwardly to himself as he continued on down the lane, the next step of his mission complete.

8

I feel like I know every inch of this cell already. The pattern of the brickwork. The places where the builders used just a bit too much mortar. Which bricks have cracked slightly. Where the whitewash on the walls is just starting to fade.

I've never been massively interested in local history, but I know this building is old. It's been a police station for years. The cells look almost Victorian, and it wouldn't surprise me if they were. I wonder how many people have been locked up in here over the years. Drunks. Drug addicts. Burglars. Murderers.

Brian told me they can only keep me for twenty-four hours. Just another twenty-two to go, then. It feels like I've been here for an age already. Before the twenty-four hours is up they'll have to either charge me or release me. He mentioned that they can apply for an extension if there are special circumstances, but told me not to worry about that. That's like telling someone not to think of a bowl of fruit.

He seemed to make out that the interview would tell us something, would force the police to show their hand. But I just came out of it even more confused. We weren't able to prove it was all just a terrible mistake. The police seemed hell-bent on thinking I killed Roger. The business with his neighbour made no sense at all. I don't know this Eric guy. Why the hell would he say he saw me coming out of Roger's house when I was sitting at home in my back garden? And what was all that about my phone?

I try to think about where it might be. I remember going to going to use my phone at work yesterday morning, but I didn't have it on me. I presumed I must have left it at home, but by the time I got back the kids were playing up and dinner needed doing, and I forgot to look for it.

But the way McKenna asked about the phone makes me wonder. Why was she so keen to find it? I mean, yeah, it's probably unusual in this day and age for someone not to carry their mobile around with them the whole time, but so what? Does she think there's going to be something on there that would incriminate me? Maybe she thinks I popped it in my calendar. *4th August: Kill Roger.*

Roger. In all of this, I've barely had the time or mental capacity to process the fact that he's actually dead.

Brendan is going to be devastated. It's only three years since we lost his mum.

Belinda and Roger were inseparable. They were the perfect parents, the perfect couple and the perfect business partnership. Their dedication to themselves, to each other and to the firm was the foundation for everything. They'd only retired six months earlier, staying on as shareholders but handing the day-to-day running of the business on to Brendan.

They'd had plans for round-the-world cruises, golf club memberships, holiday homes — you name it, they were going to do it. Belinda's diagnosis came nine days after their retirement party.

Renal cancer.

At first, they thought they'd caught it. Belinda was the sort of woman who kept an eye on her body and her health. It was still in the fairly early stages, they said. Early stage two.

They decided on surgery to remove the kidney, but by then it had started to build more aggressively. The last scan before surgery showed it had spread. Far from being an early stage two, we were now looking at full-blown stage four cancer. A terminal diagnosis.

The radiotherapy was brutal, but it gave the family some extra time with her. A few more months watching this bold, powerful matriarch wither into a shrivelled little old lady.

They never did go on their round-the-world cruise.

Brendan had been unsure about taking on the responsibility of running the business when his parents first mentioned retirement. He didn't tell them that, though.

Brendan's always been the sort of man who's happy with his lot in life. He had his house, his marriage, his kids, his job and that was all fine. The changing of the guard meant he had to step up to the plate. Order had been disrupted.

We chatted about what a great opportunity it might be. We could build on the foundations his parents had worked so hard to put in place, and potentially even take the business in a new direction. Once I'd suggested that, taking over the reins and keeping the company on its existing path seemed like the safer option. I think that's what convinced Brendan to accept his parents' offer.

Thank god Belinda isn't around to witness all this. I imagine her marching into the police station, demanding to see the Chief Constable.

If it had been any other situation, the first person I would call is Roger. He'd know exactly what to do in this situation. He'd know which solicitor to use, what to say, what to do. He was the calm, level head. The voice of experience.

But he's gone. Dead. Murdered. And the police think I killed him.

The heaving sobs start to come before I've even realised. I lie down on my blue plastic mattress, bring my knees up to my chest and let it all out.

9

'Harry, come on. We'll be late if you don't hurry up.'

It's a familiar sound on a Saturday morning in this house. Brendan's always firm but fair with the boys. He rarely raises his voice to them, and when he does they know they must have done something seriously wrong.

Most of the time, just that extra touch of sharpness lets them know it's their last chance, and they do as they're told. I wish they did that with me.

'Are you sure you don't want any breakfast?' I ask him, as he wraps his arms around me.

'I'm sure. I'll grab something while we're out.'

It's the same exchange we have every week, but I'd feel dreadful if I didn't ask. I know he's a big boy and can either make his own breakfast or go to a café, but that's not the point. It's just another part of our routine.

'Back the same sort of time as usual?' I ask.

'I imagine so. No cup matches this week, so should all end on time.'

For the last three weeks running, at least one of the boys has been involved in a cup match that's gone to extra time and penalties, adding the best part of an hour onto the day's activities. No-one ever told me that having kids meant weekends would suddenly become busier than weekdays. I always used to find it funny when people said they went to work to relax. Now I know exactly what they mean.

'Much planned for the day?' Brendan asks me, pouring himself a glass of juice.

'Nope.'

'Good,' he says. 'I'll try and take the slow route back, give you an extra few minutes. I was thinking maybe we could get a takeaway in tonight. For when the boys are in bed.'

I nod. 'That'd be nice.'

It's the same routine as every week, but it feels comforting, familiar. I think I'd be more worried if Brendan did have breakfast, or moaned at me for resting, or didn't suggest getting a takeaway. It's the little dance we do every week, and it's what makes our weekends what they are. I'm certainly not complaining.

Jacob comes bounding into the room, pleased as punch that he's totally ready to go, while Harry's still upstairs in his pyjamas.

'Jacob, boots,' Brendan says, picking him up and

depositing him back out on the mat in the hallway. 'No muddy studs inside the house, you'll wreck the carpets.'

I head upstairs to fetch Harry. He's starting to get to that age where sometimes a different style of parenting works.

'Hey,' I say, as I walk into his room and see him lying back on his bed, playing a game on his 3DS. 'Come on. You've got to get ready for football.'

'I don't feel well,' he says, shaking his head.

'How so?'

'Dunno. Just don't feel well.'

I had a feeling this might happen. Brendan didn't make a big thing of it, but he told me last week that Harry'd been given a yellow card in last week's match. Harry had thought that was really unfair — and it probably was — so he started arguing with the referee. Not wanting Harry to get sent off, the coach had substituted him and brought another boy on. To Harry, that just cemented in his mind that no-one had his back. So much for a team game, as far as he was concerned.

Brendan had spoken to him on the way back, saying the coach *did* have his back, and that's why he substituted him — to make sure he didn't get suspended for future games — but Harry wasn't having any of it. As far as he was concerned, there'd been a major injustice in showing him the yellow card in the first place, and no-one had stepped in to rectify it.

That's just one of the things I love about Harry — how principled he is. Everything has to be fair.

'Bit of fresh air might help,' I say.

'It won't.'

'It might. It'll definitely help more than lying on your bed all day. Who are you playing today?'

'Fairfields.'

'Are they any good?'

'No, they're rubbish.'

'Well there you go, then. It'll be a nice easy run out for you. Might even bag yourself a couple of goals. Besides which,' I say, snuggling up beside him, 'I have it on good authority that Dad's going to take you out to that new American diner afterwards.'

Harry looks up at me. 'Really?'

'Uh-huh. Don't tell him I told you, though.'

'Well, alright,' he says, switching off the 3DS and changing into his football kit.

I head back downstairs, to find Jacob still standing on the front doormat, bag in one hand, football under the other arm, ready and raring to go.

I try to suppress a chuckle as I walk through to the kitchen, where Brendan's gone to fetch his own shoes.

'Harry's on his way down,' I say. 'Oh, and you're going to Fat Tony's for lunch after the football.'

'What? Since when?'

'Since Harry needed bribing to even leave the house

today. It's fine — I'll have a late lunch and we'll just get the takeaway for a bit later.'

'Sure?'

'Sure.'

I'm not going to lie. The chance to get an extra hour to myself, on top of the time they'll already be out, is absolute bliss. I'm certainly not about to turn down that sort of opportunity.

A minute or so later, Harry comes down the stairs, in his full kit, ready to go. With a bit of shuffling and scuffling by the front door, it's finally open and they head out into the sunshine for their morning of fun, while I take a deep breath, hear the door close and let it back out again.

I allow myself a small smile, then I head into the kitchen to grab my book and make myself a cup of tea.

10

Eric Black had polished off the last of the cornflakes and was considering whether to pop out into the garden to do some light pruning.

The weather was due to be good, and it'd been a fair few days since he'd last been out there.

His reverie was stolen, though, by the sounds coming from next door. The first one sounded like a cross between a roar and a scream.

Although his eyesight hadn't been the best for a few years, there was no faulting his hearing. Besides which, the walls in these houses weren't exactly soundproof.

He shuffled closer to the wall to get a better angle, and heard what sounded like a pained moan, punctuated by grunts and rhythmic banging. It didn't sound right. Not at all.

He wondered about going round to check everything

was okay. This was a Neighbourhood Watch area, and Eric took his responsibilities on that front very seriously indeed.

He marched as quickly as he could through the hallway and up the stairs to his spare bedroom, where he'd have the best view of Roger's driveway. Along with Roger's own car, he could see another one parked beside it, a little closer to the house. He vaguely recognised it, but he wasn't sure where from. It would come to him eventually, he was sure.

Just as he was about to go back downstairs and listen at the wall again, he saw movement outside, then the sound of Roger's front door closing.

Yes. That's where he recognised the car from. It belonged to Roger's daughter-in-law — the woman who was now climbing into the driver's seat.

He watched as she fumbled to start the engine, before flooring the accelerator, spraying the front of Roger's house with gravel as she roared off down the road.

That certainly wasn't normal. She'd always seemed like such a nice, calm girl.

He went back downstairs as quickly as he could, and opened the front door. He made his way across to Roger's house and rang the doorbell. He gave it a few seconds, but there were no signs of movement, so he gave five strong raps on the door. Another thirty seconds, and nothing.

Eric headed back inside his house and picked the phone up from the hall table.

He looked at the laminated card that he'd placed next to the phone a few months earlier — a collection of numbers he might need to call. The fraud number for his bank, who to call if he smells gas, the number of his local Neighbourhood Watch coordinator. It also had the well-known 999 emergency number and the newfangled non-emergency number, 101.

Was this an emergency? He didn't know. It'd be a terrible inconvenience to drag the police out here if there was nothing wrong.

He decided to play it safe and call 101.

After a couple of seconds, he was greeted by an auto-mated voice, introducing the 101 non-emergency number. He was asked if he'd like to be connected to his local police force.

'Yes,' he said, feeling both daft at talking to a robot and annoyed that yet another perfectly good job had been taken over by an algorithm.

The phone rang for a few seconds, then a man answered and introduced himself.

'Uh, it's my next-door neighbour,' Eric said. 'His name is Roger.'

'Alright. And has there been some sort of incident?'

'I don't know. I think so.'

'Is Roger in some sort of danger?' the man asked.

'I don't know. I think so. I think he's just been attacked.'

'Okay, was this at his house?'

'Yes.'

'What's his address?'

'Uh, Missingham Drive. Number 42. No. Sorry. 44.'

'44 Missingham Drive?'

'Yes, sorry. I live at number 42.'

'Okay. And is his attacker still there?'

'No. She left just now.'

'Was this on foot? Could she still be in the area?'

Eric began to feel himself panic. 'No, in her car. She drove away.'

'Okay. Can you describe her car to me?'

'Uh, yes. Blue. Uh, small. Small-ish.'

'Do you know the make and model?'

'No. No, sorry. I don't know cars very well.'

'That's fine. What was it that made you think your neighbour was attacked?'

'I heard noises. It sounded like he was in pain. And someone was grunting and banging. Then I came and looked out of the window and she ran out of the house and sped off in her car. Then I knocked at the door and there was no answer.'

'Okay. We'll send officers to take a look. Did you see the attacker going into the property?'

'Uh, no. No, I didn't.'

'So you didn't see how many went in?'

'No,' Eric said, now starting to see what the call handler was getting at.

'Okay. I'd ask you not to try to enter the property, then. Stay in your own house until the police arrive. It's possible someone could still be in there.'

Eric gulped. He hadn't thought of it like that. This just wasn't the sort of thing that happened on Missingham Drive.

11

There tended to be a bit of a pattern to these calls. There was an unbelievably high number of domestic disputes — either someone calling the police because his neighbour had parked across his drive or trimmed his hedge without permission, or a wife calling the police on her husband because he'd hidden the remote control and wouldn't tell her where it was.

Before Stuart Houghton joined the police, he'd read these stories in newspapers and assumed they must be fairly rare occurrences — something that happened in one police force once every few months. He was wrong. Most days, he'd spend his time wondering why the hell half the people he went out to see had even called the police.

His favourite had to be the guy who flagged them down on the high street because he'd just been to get a takeaway kebab and they'd put fried onions on it, even though he specifically asked them not to. The guy was livid, and thought flagging down a police car was perfectly justified.

And that was the rub of it. It wasn't about what any reasonable person thought was a crime — it was what the aggrieved person judged was a crime. As far as they were concerned, the police were there for them and that was the end of that.

Oftentimes, it'd be a case of having to explain calmly that this was a civil dispute and that the police only got involved in criminal matters; or that no, it wasn't technically illegal to hide the remote control because you're not too keen on Emmerdale.

What was vital, though, was that the public didn't lose faith in the police and choose not to call them when they really needed them — when a crime actually had been committed.

All he knew about the call they were on their way to now was that a man had called in to say he heard a commotion next door and was subsequently unable to get a response when checking the neighbour was okay. There was no evidence of any injury or crime having been committed, but it was always best to check.

It could have been a regular, everyday argument and the guy could've just gone out in the garden or popped into the shower afterwards, and that's why he didn't answer the door. Maybe he didn't like his neighbour and was deliberately avoiding speaking to him. There was a multitude of possibilities — all of which Stuart had seen a hundred times before.

This call, though, had been graded as immediate response, meaning they had a target attendance time of fifteen minutes. They weren't too far off that target — there wasn't anything else they could have done, having been on the blues-and-twos from the moment they received the call.

His colleague, Julie Hutchinson, pulled up outside 44 Missingham Drive and switched off the engine. She was a good twenty years or so older than him, and had been in the job since he was at primary school — something she liked to remind him of regularly. He wondered why she'd never gone for promotion or moved into a more specialised policing job. It certainly wasn't due to her work ethic or eye for detail. She was one of the finest officers he'd ever worked with.

They were barely halfway up the driveway before the front door to number 42 opened, and an older man came out in his slippers.

'What sort of time do you call this?' he asked.

That was a pretty common reaction. Most members of the public didn't understand that all calls were graded, and that they could only send officers to a scene if there were officers available. When there were usually a maximum of six officers to cover an area around thirty miles wide, it was unlikely you'd have someone rocking up within five minutes — unless you were very lucky. Stuart could have bet his bottom dollar that, come the next election, this guy would blindly vote for the same government that had slashed staff numbers and decimated the policing budget to the point where the country was on the verge of civil anarchy.

'We were the closest unit and we came as quickly as we possibly could, sir,' Julie replied, trying to be as polite as possible to the small little Welsh man who stood in front of her. 'Can you tell us what's happened, please?'

'Well, I can't get any answer at the door.'

'Your neighbour's door?'

'Yes. I was in my kitchen, having just finished my breakfast. I was wondering whether or not to go outside and do some weeding, when I heard this almighty noise from next door.'

'What sort of noise?'

'A sort of banging, I suppose. Grunting. I can't really describe it, but it just didn't sound right to me. I wondered if maybe he was having some work done, so I popped upstairs and looked out of the spare bedroom window in case there was a tradesman's van. And I saw the woman coming out of the house, get into her car and speed off down the road.'

'A woman?' Julie asked.

'Yes, that's right.'

'And this was at what time?'

'Oh, blimey. About half an hour ago now. There's no

use running down the road after her, if that's what you're asking me.'

Stuart went next door to have a look through the windows and see if he could spot anything unusual inside.

'And did you pick anything up from her body language? What sort of state was she in?' Julie asked Eric.

'A right old state, if you ask me. She practically ran out, slammed the car door and sped right off the drive. Didn't even look to see if any traffic was coming. Not that we get much traffic up here, mind. Not since they put that new bypass in. Been an absolute godsend, that has. Did you know, before they put the bypass in we used to get an average of one hundred and eighty cars an hour along this road? That's one every twenty seconds. Right little rat run, it was. They reckon now it's more like twenty an hour. That's one every three minutes. Much more tolerable, if you ask me.'

Julie forced a smile. 'So she was panicked, would you say?'

'Oh yes, I'd say. Looked like they'd had a right old barney. That's why I popped over to see if Roger was alright. When I couldn't get any answer, I decided to call the police.'

'Julie,' Stuart called, rounding the corner onto the driveway once again. 'Side gate was unlocked. I peered through the kitchen window. You got a sec?'

12

EARLIER THAT MORNING, 9.40 AM.

Stuart stood back, lifted his leg and aimed the sole of his boot at the back door's lock.

It took four solid kicks before it split and allowed him to push his way through and into the kitchen.

Julie called on her radio for immediate police backup and an ambulance.

Stuart, thinking he might have detected a very faint pulse, carefully laid Roger on the floor and began to perform CPR.

Julie stepped back outside to speak to Eric.

'Is he okay?' he asked, before Julie could even say a word.

'We're doing what we can.'

'Oh god. He's not, is he? I can see his legs. I can see the blood. Oh god.'

Julie took Eric to one side, out of sight of the kitchen.

'This woman you saw leaving earlier. Can you describe her or the car for me?'

'Uh, I don't know. She's kind of... nice looking. I guess. Young, you know.'

'Young? How young?'

'Oh god, I don't know. It's so difficult to tell these days.'

'Younger than me?' Julie asked.

'Oh my, yes.'

Julie tried not to look offended. 'And what about the car? Do you know what make and model it was?'

'No, no I don't. Is he going to be okay? Roger, I mean. Will he pull through?'

'We hope so. My colleague's doing everything he can, and the paramedics are on their way.'

'Has she killed him?'

'We're hoping not. But we do need to find her, I hope you understand that.'

Eric seemed to steel himself slightly. 'Yes, yes, of course.'

'So the car. You don't remember seeing a badge at all? Was it a big car? Small one?'

'They're all getting bigger these days. Some of them are enormous great tractors compared to what we used to have when I was younger. Can I see him? Maybe I can try talking to him, get him to come round a bit.'

'I'm afraid not, no. We need to keep the area secured as a crime scene. Even if he's fine, there's been at least a very serious assault which will need investigating. Now, I need you to concentrate for me. My colleague is taking good care of Roger. I need you to help me with some information so we can catch whoever did this. Does that make sense?'

Eric swallowed and nodded. 'Yes, yes. Perfect sense.'

Julie wasn't so sure. 'Okay, good. What colour was the car she drove away in?'

'Uh, blue, I think. Yes, blue.'

'Okay. Dark blue? Light blue?'

Eric shook his head. 'No, just blue.'

'Right. Okay. And was it smaller than most cars? One of the big ones?'

'It was on the smaller side, I suppose. Not tiny by any means, but not one of the massive ones.'

'So a medium-sized blue car?'

'That's the one, yes. Do you know it?'

Julie looked at him for a moment. 'I don't think so, no. What about the woman herself? How would you describe her, physically speaking?'

'Well… she's sort of slender. Long hair.'

'What colour hair?'

'Light. Blonde, I suppose you'd call it.'

'And is there anything else you can remember?'

Eric seemed to think for a moment, then shook his head. 'No. No, that's all I know.'

Julie asked Eric to wait round the front of the house to guide any backup vehicles or ambulance response units in, while she radioed in the details she'd been given.

'We're looking for a medium-sized blue car — no further details at this moment — driven by a young, blonde woman of slim build,' she said, putting the call out for backup. 'We'll try to get more specific details, but it's not looking promising at this stage.'

She stepped into the kitchen to see how Stuart was getting on.

'I don't think we're getting anything,' he said. 'I'm pretty sure he's gone.'

Julie sighed. 'You know what they'll say, Stu. Pretty sure's not sure enough.'

'What's the point?' he said. 'The bloke's head's been caved in. He's gone.'

'I know. But you've got to protect your own arse. You don't want to be going through the investigations and disciplinaries after this. Trust me.'

IT WAS ALMOST ten o'clock by the time the paramedics had arrived, done their bit and finally declared life extinct. Two colleagues were on the front drive, consoling a blood-covered Stuart, who'd now be scarred for life at the memory of having to spend twenty minutes trying to bring a dead man back to life.

Julie had known colleagues who'd had to do similar

things. One of them had attended a suicide, where a man had thrown himself off the top of a multi-storey car park. The overriding responsibility to save life, plus the pressure of hordes of people watching, meant he'd been obliged to carry out CPR in order to try and save the man's life. It had been completely futile. The guy was practically liquidised the moment he hit the pavement. But the instruction to try at all costs had been beaten into him so hard during his training, and the pressure of a watching public meant he felt he had no choice in the matter.

That officer had been traumatised by nightmares and flashbacks, and doctors eventually diagnosed him with post-traumatic stress disorder. He never worked again. Eighteen months later, he ended his own life.

Julie was keen to make sure Stuart didn't go the same way. She'd make it her personal duty to ensure he was looked after and given the care and treatment he was going to need. Stu was a tough cookie, but even the toughest of cookies crumbled under that sort of pressure.

She watched as the paramedics brought Roger's body down the side passage and lifted it into the ambulance, before driving off without their sirens on.

13

Stuart had been taken away from the scene by colleagues, but Julie had decided to stay at the scene with the other officers.

She was certain there was more to be had from the neighbour, Eric Black. She didn't think he was deliberately hiding anything from her, but she had a good sense of when a witness had more than a passing familiarity with a suspect.

She sat down in his living room with him and a young PC she'd not met before, and watched as Eric spooned four sugars into his tea, before slurping at it.

'Eric, I know you're obviously very upset and it's been a very traumatic morning for you, but the first hour or two gives us the best chance of catching whoever did this. And you're the person who can help us.'

Eric shook his head. 'I've told you everything I know.'

Julie ignored his protestations. 'So, to recap. You saw a medium-sized blue car, is that right?'

'Yes.'

'You don't know the make or model?'

'No.'

'And had you seen this car before?' Julie asked.

'That specific car, or just that type of car?'

'That specific one. Or any car which could have been that one, parked up at Roger's house in the past.'

Eric seemed to think for a moment. 'Well, yes.'

Bingo. This was exactly why Julie wanted to press him further.

'When?'

'Uh, quite often. Maybe once every few weeks. Sometimes less.'

'Do you remember any part of the car's registration number at all?'

Eric thought for a moment, then shook his head. 'No. Not at all.'

'What about the age? Do you remember the two numbers in the middle of the registration? Maybe the three letters at the end?'

'No, sorry. I don't have a very good memory for things like that. And in any case I wouldn't have been able to see the plate without my glasses on.'

'And what about the woman?' Julie asked. 'Was she usually in the car?'

'Oh, yes. And sometimes in the other one, too.'

Julie raised her eyebrows, her interest piqued. 'The other one?'

'Yes, there's a black car too. One of those big ones, you know. Like a tractor.'

'A four-by-four?'

'Yes, that's the one.'

'Do you know the make and model of that one?'

Eric very suddenly lost his temper. 'Oh for Christ's sake, no. I don't know cars. I don't know how many times I need to keep telling you this.'

Julie could tell when she was perhaps pushing things too far, but she knew she was close to picking up a golden nugget. The fact he'd seen the suspect before, and that she had a second car, was entirely new information and she felt sure there was more still to come.

'Okay, sorry. And I presume you don't know the registration number of the big black vehicle either?'

Eric looked her in the eye and spoke firmly. 'No.'

'Alright. And was she always on her own in this car?'

'Sometimes if she was in the blue one. The black one, no. He usually drives the black one. And most of the time they've got the kids with them.'

Julie blinked a few times. 'Sorry, who's "he"? And the kids?'

'Her husband. And their little ones. Who else did you think I meant?'

Julie shuffled slightly in her seat. 'Sorry, I think I've missed something. Do you know these people?'

'Oh, no. Not personally.'

'But do you know who she is? The woman you saw driving away this morning?'

'Well, I can't tell you much. All I can tell you is she's Roger's daughter-in-law.'

Julie had to physically stop her jaw from dropping. Over forty minutes they'd been here now, and it was well over an hour since Roger had been attacked and the suspect had fled, and this guy picks *now* to tell the police who she is?

'Do you know her first name?' Julie asked.

Eric shook his head. 'No. Sorry.'

'What about the husband? Children, perhaps? Roger must have mentioned their names at some point.'

'Well, no. He's not lived there that long. He downsized and moved here after his wife died, see. I don't know. I suppose I've never asked. They sort of keep themselves to themselves.'

'Excuse me for a minute,' she said to her colleague, stepping out of the room.

She put a call out on her radio. 'We have some new information regarding the suspect. It's believed she's the daughter-in-law of the deceased. No full name at this point, but we presume the surname is Walker.'

Julie looked at her watch. It was now getting on for 10.15. With any luck, the on-duty SIO would be there shortly to take control of the investigation. She couldn't take any chances, though. She called into the control room and asked them give her authorisation to start going door-to-door. She felt sure that someone, somewhere in this street must know the woman's name.

14

EARLIER THAT MORNING, 10.15 AM.

For Julie, this was one of the worst parts of the job. Most of her colleagues hated doing paperwork or collating information back at the office, but she didn't mind that. More often than not, it was something that helped solve a crime or take a case on to the next stage.

Door-to-door enquiries tended to follow a fairly predictable pattern. Most people wouldn't be in. That took a significant dent out of the potential witness pool. Of those who did answer their doors, the majority would just shake their heads and give her a blank stare, as if she'd asked them to solve the Hodge conjecture. Those who did have something to say, would usually say something entirely useless and unrelated to the enquiry.

Of course, there were times when door-to-door and telephone enquiries threw up some gold nuggets, but it was rare. The reason it was done so often was because it was free, relatively easy and tended to reveal information which the police might not have been aware of otherwise.

There was no answer from the first three houses Julie knocked at on Missingham Drive. It was August, so many people would be away on holiday. It was also a sunny Saturday, so those who weren't on holiday would be out somewhere else, enjoying the sunshine and doing whatever it was normal people did at the weekend.

The fourth house she knocked at was across the road and a couple of doors further down. A young-ish woman opened the door. Julie could hear the sound of children playing noisily inside.

She introduced herself and asked if the woman had seen anything odd going on across the road that morning.

'No, I don't think so. To be honest, though, I've not really been looking. I've been in the kitchen sorting stuff out for the barbecue. We've got a few friends over later.'

Julie smiled. She could just about remember what it was like to socialise.

'Well there's been a serious incident that's occurred, so if anything does pop into your mind, can you give me a call?' Julie handed her a card, which had the local police force's logo, her name and rank and her contact details.

'Oh right. Yeah, okay,' the woman said, her tone changing perceptibly.

'While I'm here,' Julie said, trying to make it sound like a casual afterthought, 'I don't suppose you know anything about Roger Walker's family, do you?'

'Like what? He lives on his own, I think. His wife died a couple of years back.'

'What about other family? Do they come to visit at all?'

'Oh yeah, they do. He's got a son. Brendan, I think it is. My other half went to school with him.'

'Oh really?' Julie replied, trying not to sound too enthusiastic. Although this woman could be a fantastic source of information, Julie was aware that some people were very protective over their communities. If they thought the information they gave was likely to get someone they knew into trouble, they tended to shut up shop pretty quickly. 'Do you know the rest of the family's names?'

The woman pushed her lips out and shook her head. 'No, don't think so. Steve might know. One sec.'

The woman stepped back into the house and disappeared into the kitchen. A couple of seconds later, a man stepped into view, wiping his hands on a dishcloth.

'Do you remember what your old mate Brendan's missus is called? The one whose dad lives across the road,' the woman said.

The man looked at Julie for a moment. 'Uh, Amy I think. Yeah, Amy. Why?'

'There was an incident at one of your neighbours' houses earlier on this morning, and we just need to try and get as much information and context as we can. Did you see or hear anything at all?'

The man did the same pushing-out of the lip and shake of the head his partner had done only moments earlier. 'No, don't think so, did we?' he asked her.

'No, sorry. Why, what happened anyway? Is Roger alright?'

'We're not sure yet,' Julie said, trying to skirt around the question. She had some more things she needed to ask before she was able to pull the shutters down on this one. 'Do Brendan and Amy visit regularly?'

'Yeah, pretty regularly,' the man said, throwing the dishcloth onto his shoulder and leaning against the hall wall. 'They usually come together with the kids, but there'll quite often be one of them on their own. At least once a week, I'd say.'

His partner nodded her agreement.

'Do they live locally?'

'I'm not sure,' the man said. 'I don't imagine they can be far away. Brendan used to live in town when he was growing up. We went to school together. But I've not spoken to him since.'

'Are you friends on Facebook or anything like that?'

'Nah. I don't really use it, to be honest. Got too much going on.'

Julie nodded. If only more people were like him. 'But you think they still live locally?'

'Well, yeah. They're over here a fair bit and I've seen them around town before, so I don't think they live far away.

Julie nodded. 'Do you know what sort of car they drive?'

The man's eyes flicked upwards and he raised his eyebrows. 'Uh, they've got a black Range Rover. That's the one they usually turn up in. But sometimes if it's just her and the kids she's got a blue Fiesta, or it might be a Focus. One of those.'

Julie tried to hide her excitement. 'I don't suppose you know the reg numbers, do you?'

The man shook his head. 'No idea, I'm afraid.'

Julie smiled. 'Alright, not to worry. I'll get one of my colleagues to pop in shortly and take a statement, if that's alright? I just need to make a quick call.'

'Oh right. Yeah. Okay,' the man said, seemingly thrown off balance. 'What's happened, then? Is everything alright?'

But Julie was already halfway down their garden path, relaying the information over the radio.

15

Julie could barely contain her excitement. Just a little bit of old-fashioned policing had netted her the suspect's full name and the make and model of the car she was driving.

She'd radioed into the control room before she'd even properly thanked the couple across the road or got their names.

'Need you to check the voters' register for me, please,' she said, speaking to the officer in the control room.

'Okay, go ahead,' came the response.

'I need details of any Amy Walkers living locally. Walker is Whiskey Alpha Lima Kilo Echo Romeo.'

'Alright. How local?'

'Not sure. Try ten mile radius.'

'Okay, two seconds… Sorry, system's on the go slow this morning.'

Julie raised her eyebrows. The sodding systems were always on the go slow, and particularly so when she needed to access some information on them.

'Ah, right. Here we are. It's showing five within those parameters. Do you want details?'

'Yes please.'

He read out the list of addresses, and Julie wrote them all down in her notebook. Then she thanked him and ended the call.

By now, the on-call senior investigating officer had arrived at the scene. Detective Inspector Jane McKenna was the sort of woman who took no prisoners. She didn't do niceties, unless it was in her best interest to do so.

'I've got something that might be useful,' Julie said, approaching McKenna. 'Neighbour over the road has identified the suspect as Amy Walker. Says she drives a blue Ford Fiesta or Focus, which matches the description given by the witness. We've checked the voters' register and there are five Amy Walkers within a ten-mile radius.'

She handed the notebook to McKenna, who nodded and smiled.

'Great work. I'll get officers allocated to these addresses. With any luck we'll have her back at the big blue hotel before lunchtime.'

16

EARLIER THAT MORNING, 10.45AM.

PC Jason Day stopped the car and put the handbrake on. This was the second Amy Walker they'd been asked to attend, having been less than a minute's drive away from the first when the call came in.

It seemed like a nice area, and it wasn't somewhere Jason had been called to before. It was a pretty lane, with houses dotted either side of it every now and again, none of them close enough to be visible to the neighbours, but not quite giving it a completely rural feel.

His colleague, Pete Briers, gave his usual grunt as he pulled himself out of the car and onto the pavement.

'Here you are, Jase,' he said, gesturing at the driveway of the address they'd been given. Sitting on the tarmac, seemingly untouched, was a blue Ford Fiesta.

'Could be it,' Jason said, radioing into the control room. 'Yeah, we've got a positive ID on a car,' he said, into the radio. 'Registration Foxtrot Oscar One Seven, Uniform Tango Alpha. It's a blue Ford Fiesta, over.'

'Received. One moment, over.'

The wait was almost agonising. This had to be the right Amy Walker. It'd be a shame to have to spend the next couple of hours booking her into custody and filling out all the resulting paperwork when they could be out and about on this sunny Saturday, but an arrest was an arrest.

The call would now be going out to a sergeant or above at the murder scene, who'd likely give instructions to arrest this Amy Walker. An arrest for murder wasn't the sort of thing they could do lightly.

Twenty seconds later, the response came over the radio.

'Okay, go ahead and arrest.'

Jason and Pete walked up the driveway and Pete rang the doorbell. Jason, meanwhile, put the back of his hand on the bonnet of the Fiesta. It was hot, but then again so was the rest of the car. The blistering August sunshine had probably warmed up every car in the area, so the warmth was no sure indication that the car had recently been used.

After a short while, it became clear there was no answer at the door. Jason walked round to the side of the house, but couldn't see any signs of life inside.

Pete went to the front window and knocked, hoping he might be able to get a response.

Just as Jason was about to jump the gate, he saw movement inside, and came back round to the front of the house just in time to see the front door open.

'Good morning. We're looking for a Mrs Amy Walker,' Pete said, looking over the woman's shoulder and into the house, keeping aware of any potential weapons or other people in the house.

'Uh, yes. That's me,' the woman said. 'What's happened?'

Jason nodded. They'd already agreed in advance that this would be his nick. 'Amy Walker, I'm arresting you on suspicion of murder. You do not have to say anything. But, it may harm your defence if you do not mention when questioned something which you later rely on in court. Anything you do say may be given in evidence.'

17

It's hard to sleep in a place like this, but there's not a whole lot else I can do. If I try to stay awake, my brain takes over with all sorts of thoughts.

I try to remain level-headed and logical. I know I just need to let this take its course. We're always told we can trust the justice system to come good in the end. I just hope the end is close.

I've been doing some relaxation techniques to try and sleep, or at least keep my mind clear and relaxed. Getting worked up and emotional isn't going to help — I know that — but it's easier said than done.

The shouting and yelling from the nearby cells makes it a lot harder to keep calm. Judging by the noise, I'm guessing there's been some sort of football-related violence.

As I try to block it out, I'm jolted by the sound of my cell door opening.

'Amy?' the officer says. 'Detective Inspector wants to speak with you again. I'll take you through to Interview Room 1.'

What surprised me most about being in here is how nice the officers at the bottom of the rung have been. The uniformed PCs have been checking on me, seeing if I was hungry or thirsty and generally treating me like an actual human being. Perhaps they've not yet progressed far enough up the career ladder to forget that people are innocent until proven guilty in this country. Shame I can't say the same for McKenna.

The interview room is starting to feel like a boxing ring. One where I sit huddled in the corner, taking every punch that's thrown at me, desperately waiting for the referee to end the match for my own safety.

DI McKenna starts the recording equipment, which emits its long, piercing beep.

'Okay, Amy. We just wanted to follow up with a few more questions and to try and get some context as to what happened earlier today. Are you alright with that?'

'Fine. How's Brendan? And how are the boys?' I ask.

'They're being given all the support we can give them,' she tells me, with a look that adds *no thanks to you* on the end without needing to be said. 'Happy to start?' she asks.

'Yeah.'

Brian gives me a look that tells me any other answers should be 'no comment'. I'm starting to get used to decoding his facial twitches now.

'Okay. So in our last interview you opted not to comment when we asked you where you'd been this morning. Why was that?'

I look at Brian. 'No comment.'

'Did you visit Roger?'

'No comment.'

'Was it something to do with work, perhaps? He's a shareholder in the company you work for, isn't he? The company run by your husband. Did you go to see him for work reasons?'

'Detective Inspector, my client has not admitted to going to the deceased's house this morning, so I find your line of questioning misleading,' Brian interjects.

'I'm simply trying to find out why she might have gone to visit Roger Walker,' McKenna replies.

'And until she tells you she did, or until you can provide some evidence that she did, this is merely an allegation.'

A smile starts to break across McKenna's face. 'Alright. Not a problem. Amy, do you recall receiving a text message from Roger yesterday afternoon, asking you to come and see him this morning?'

I look at her, then at Brian. There was no text message. I didn't even have my phone yesterday — I got to work and realised I didn't have it, and thought I must have left it at home. By the time I got home the boys were kicking off and shouting and screaming, and I forgot all about it. I barely use the thing anyway.

'No comment,' I say, trusting Brian, but desperately wanting to explain my side of the story to McKenna.

'Perhaps if I read you the message verbatim it'll jog your memory,' she says. '"Hi Amy. Just wondered if you could pop over tomorrow morning for an hour or so. Wanted to go through some work stuff with you." That was the message we obtained from Roger's phone. Does it ring any bells?'

I swallow, desperate to answer, desperate to tell them I never received any such message, but the look on Brian's face is unmoving.

'No comment.'

'I mean, presumably it must do. Because you replied twenty-six minutes later saying, "Yes, no problem. Will be there for 9."'

I'm shaking. I didn't send any text messages yesterday. I haven't sent any for days. I didn't even have my phone yesterday.

'When?' I ask, my voice squeaking slightly.

'When were the messages sent?' McKenna asks.

I nod.

'Roger's initial text to you was sent at 16.01, and your reply was sent at 16.27.'

Four o'clock in the afternoon, then just before half-past. While I was at work. While I thought my phone was at home. While it was lost.

'No. No, that wasn't me.'

'Does anyone else have access to your phone?'

'No, just me,' I answer quickly. 'I told you, I lost my phone. I didn't even have it, so how the hell could I have sent any messages?'

Brian puts his hand on my arm.

'Does your phone have a passcode on it?' McKenna asks. 'Or any sort of fingerprint recognition?'

Brian taps my arm and leans in to whisper into my ear. 'If it does, don't answer them. Go no comment.'

'No comment,' I say. I didn't set up the fingerprint recognition system because I don't trust it — don't want my fingerprints on record — but I do have a passcode. It's my year of birth.

'So if nobody else has access to your phone, would I be right in assuming that nobody else could have sent that text message?'

My jaw is aching from how hard I'm clenching my jaw. 'No comment,' I say, through gritted teeth.

McKenna nods slowly. 'Do you and your husband own a claw hammer, Amy?'

My eyes narrow as I try to work out why she's asking me this. 'No comment,' I say.

'Only most people do, I'd say. I'd go so far as to say it's probably the basic tool most people have, apart from screwdrivers. Would you agree?'

'No comment.'

'The Scenes of Crime Officers believe Roger may have been killed with a claw hammer. The officers searching your house have checked the toolbox and the garage, but can't seem to find a claw hammer. Is yours missing at all? Lost, perhaps? You do seem to lose things quite a lot.'

Brian interjects. 'Detective Inspector, if you have some evidence that my client's hypothetical claw hammer was used in the attack on Roger Walker, please provide it. Otherwise, it would be wise to note that an absence does not constitute proof of anything.'

There's silence for a couple of moments before McKenna speaks again.

'When did you lose your phone, Amy?'

I last saw it on Thursday night, I think, but I stick to what I've been told to say. 'No comment.'

'Alright. So you've told us you didn't send that text message to Roger. And in our last interview you told us that you'd lost your phone. But we've just ascertained that no-one else would have had access to your phone in order to send that text message. Do you want to say anything about that?'

I swallow. Hard. 'No comment.'

'Amy, have you ever heard of cell site triangulation?'

Brian narrows his eyes and looks at me.

'No comment,' I say. I haven't.

'Effectively, all mobile phones get their signals from

nearby towers, or masts. Usually, you're not connected to just one tower, but to multiple ones. Your mobile phone sort of "reaches out" to these towers. Each tower can tell which direction your phone is sending its signal from, and it can work out the distance your phone is from the tower by looking at the delay time it takes for the signal to bounce back. Are you with me?'

I am. 'No comment.'

'The more towers your phone's connected to, the more accurate we can be in pinpointing exactly where a mobile phone is located. You live in a fairly rural area, don't you?'

'No comment.'

'The signal's not great there, I know. If you're in the house you might have trouble connecting to more than one tower, but sometimes the signal improves. Your father-in-law's house is more suburban, isn't it?'

'No comment.'

'Signal's pretty good there. I imagine you'd probably be connected to a few masts.

'Detective Inspector, can I ask what you're trying to achieve here, please?' Brian asks. 'Because this sort of hedging and dancing isn't doing anyone any favours.'

McKenna smiles at him. 'Amy, cell site triangulation shows that your phone was at home all day on Friday. Or, at least, it was within approximately fifty yards of your house. It doesn't leave that location until just before 8.50 this morning. The next place it stays for any period of time is at your father-in-law's house, at one minute to nine. How long would you say it takes to get to Roger's house from yours?'

I'm physically shaking now. 'No comment.'

'What, ten minutes or so? The phone stays there for approximately three minutes, then it's on the move again. It retraces its route almost exactly, back to the approximate area of your house. Do you want to comment on that?'

I shake my head. 'No comment.'

'And that's where it's still showing now. Amy, we've got search teams at your house. It's a Saturday evening and I'm sure they're as keen to get home as I am. Do you want to save us all some time and tell us where it is?'

18

'But it wasn't me!' I yell at Brian, as he attempts to debrief me in the consultation room, following the interview.

'The problem is, you have no alibi for today. Cell site triangulation only shows that your phone was at those locations. It doesn't prove conclusively that *you* were. If we can prove you were elsewhere, even at any point during those timeframes, that'll throw doubt on the whole issue of the phone.'

'But I don't have anything,' I say, my whole body feeling weak and battered.

'Let's look at the Friday. The police have said that your phone is showing as being at home for the whole day. But you were at work, right?'

'Yeah.'

'Roger's text message was sent to you at four o'clock,

and you… your phone… replied just before four thirty. What time were you at work until?'

There's a momentary flash of excitement, then the crushing realisation. 'It was a Friday. I finish early on Fridays.'

'What time?'

'Quarter past three.'

'Okay. What time would you have been home by?'

'Uh, I went straight to the school to pick the boys up. I usually get there about half past, just as they're coming out. The rest of the week they go home with one of our neighbours who's got a daughter at the school. I pick them up when I get home around five.'

'But what time would you have been home by on Friday?'

I shake my head. '3.45, 3.50 latest.'

'And did you leave the house again?'

I sigh. 'No. The next time I went anywhere I was in the back of a police car this morning.'

'Mmmmm,' Brian murmurs.

'What?'

'Well, it's not looking particularly positive. That's all. Are they likely to find this phone of yours?'

I look at him, my eyes narrowing. 'How the fuck should I know?'

'Okay. I'm only asking. I need to know everything if I'm going to be able to help you.'

'I've told you everything. That is everything I know.

Trust me, I know as much about this as you do. Everything is new to me. The first I've heard of any of this was when the police told me, and when they told you.'

Brian shuffles awkwardly in his seat.

'The problem is, things are beginning to stack up. They've placed you at the scene. The witness evidence from the neighbour probably wouldn't be enough on its own — a smart brief would easily convince the jury the guy was old, his eyesight was failing, he might've been mistaken, he was too far away to be certain. All of that stuff and more. And the cell site triangulation isn't enough on its own either. All that proves is that your phone was there. It doesn't mean you were. But put the two together...'

'And what?' I ask, hearing myself get more and more aggressive. 'Put the two together and what?'

'...and it's starting to get to the point where it would be very difficult to convince a jury that you weren't there.'

I look at him and blink a few times. 'But I wasn't. There has to be some way we can prove that. What about forensics? They took all those swabs from me. Presumably they're trying to find out if his skin was under my nails, or if I had his blood on me or whatever. That'll show I wasn't there.'

'Absence of evidence isn't evidence of absence, I'm afraid. Just because it doesn't prove you were there, it doesn't automatically prove that you weren't.'

'But if I'd killed him there'd be forensic evidence.

There'd have to be. If there isn't any, surely that proves I couldn't have done it.'

'Doesn't quite work like that, I'm afraid.'

'But you told me it was up to the police to prove I did it. That it wasn't up to me to prove I didn't.'

Brian nods. 'True, but they're starting to stack up evidence on their side. As far as I can see it, we've got nothing on ours.'

'But their evidence is all wrong! It's being misinterpreted.'

Brian shrugs. 'What can I say? The law's an ass.'

I stand up and start pacing the small room. 'No. No, that's not good enough. I didn't do anything, Brian! We have to do something. You have to get me out of here.'

'Amy, sit down, please. It's no use getting worked up.'

When he says that, I want to throttle him or punch him in the face. Were I a violent person, I might well have done. Maybe that's one of his tactics to find out whether I'm innocent or guilty. Rile me and get me worked up and see if I snap.

'Amy, listen to me. They'll be searching your house as we speak. Sooner or later they'll find that phone. Then they can get their digital forensics people to look through it and they'll be able to see everything on there. They'll go through the rest of the house with a level of meticulousness you wouldn't believe. They'll speak to friends, family, neighbours. They'll do whatever they can to build an even stronger case against you. It's already on a knife-edge, and anything else will just tip the whole thing over in their favour. Sooner or later, we need to think smart and try for damage limitation.'

I look at him. 'What are you saying?'

'I'm saying that we might not have the option of having you walk free from here today. As things stand, the Crown Prosecution Service may well consider that the police have enough evidence to charge you. And that's when all hell breaks loose. That's when they really dig in and pile up the evidence in order to try and convince a jury. This is a murder charge. That carries a minimum fifteen year term. If they can show you took a weapon or went equipped, you're talking twenty-five years plus. If they can prove it was done for gain, to obstruct or interfere with the course of justice or if it was otherwise aggravated, the starting point is thirty years.'

I feel my breath catch in my throat. I can't face thirty years in prison. I can't even face another hour in my police cell.

'Any evidence of planning or premeditation, concealment, anything like that will only increase the sentence. Now, if this all starts to look like a real possibility, we can limit the damage. If we can show an intention to harm rather than kill, some sort of provocation, evidence of self-defence or that it wasn't premeditated, those are all mitigating factors. Without the intention to kill or the premeditation, we're potentially looking at a manslaughter charge instead. Presuming we're not talking about diminished responsibility on mental health grounds, which I think we'd find very difficult to achieve — and in any case shouldn't need — we're looking at ten years or under.'

'Ten years?'

'Possibly less. You've no criminal record, you have children waiting for you at home, you're an upstanding member of the community who was provoked and defended herself and didn't mean to kill him. You're unlikely to pose any threat to the wider community.'

'But none of that happened! I wasn't even there!' I yell.

'And if we can prove that, great. But we can't. So unless there's any evidence which is going to suddenly and miraculously come to light that can prove you weren't there, that's our best-case scenario.'

'Ten years? You're telling me ten years in prison is the best I can hope for? Missing a *decade* of my children's lives? Because of something I didn't even do?'

'I think we can push for less. And you'd likely be eligible for parole in half that.'

'Brian, I didn't do it. I didn't do anything. I'm not serving time in prison for something I didn't do!'

Brian's eyebrows flick upwards momentarily, and he cocks his head. 'You might not have much choice.'

19

Brian's words have been ringing round my head ever since I came back to my cell.

Ten years.

Eligible for parole.

You might not have much choice.

This has all suddenly become normal talk. I think back to my life before that knock at the door. It was only hours ago, but it seems like an age. This world is so far removed from the home life and routine I know. Is this going to become my new normal?

I don't know if it's because my brain is protecting me by assuming that this *is* the new normal or because I've always had faith in the criminal justice system, but I seem to have developed an odd conformity to everything that's going on. It's almost as if I know I can't change the situation, so I'm just going to have to ride it out.

My cell door opens and a police officer tells me DI McKenna wants to speak with me again in the interview room. This must be one of their tactics — get you in, ask a few questions, plant a few seeds, shit you up and put you back in your cell for a few hours. I don't know if it usually works, but all it's doing is getting me more annoyed and aggravated.

She goes through her usual routine of sitting us down, starting the recording equipment and introducing herself, DS Brennan, Brian and me.

'Amy, I know you've been advised to go no comment by your solicitor, but I would personally advise you that it might be a good idea to offer your side of the story. Judges and juries don't tend to look to favourably on defendants who no comment their way through the interview process.'

Brian, as I thought he might, interjected. 'DI McKenna, will you please stop trying to intimidate my client with talk of court cases. I know what you're doing with words like "judge", "jury" and "defendant", and it would be worth me pointing out that courts don't take that sort of police intimidation lightly, either. Unless you're planning to charge my client and attempt to progress this matter towards a court case, I'd appreciate it if you could steer away from mere speculation.'

I can imagine Brian would be quite a formidable person to have on your side in court. I don't imagine he'd actually get to that point, though. Don't barristers or senior lawyers of some sort tend to represent people in court? I don't know. And the crushing realisation that I know far less about the legal system than I thought I did fills me with dread.

McKenna ignores Brian's comments.

'The reason we wanted to speak with you again, Amy, is that in the search of your property we discovered a black iPhone 7 Plus wrapped in a cloth and shoved behind the radiator in your downstairs toilet. Do you recognise it at all?'

McKenna shows me a photograph of a mobile phone on top of a cream and pale orange patterned rag.

I look up at Brian, but get no sense of what he's thinking. As impressive as his interview room patter is, he's not exactly helped me so far. I've gone from being the victim of an entirely innocent mix-up to staring down the barrel of at least a decade in prison.

I decide to talk.

'I don't know.'

'Could it be yours?' McKenna asks.

'I don't know. It looks similar.'

Brian leans across. 'You don't need to answer these questions,' he says.

'I do. I haven't done anything wrong, and I want to get out of here as quickly as I can,' I say to him, before turning to McKenna. 'I don't know anything about any phone behind any radiator. I lost my phone a couple of days ago, and I haven't seen it since. I don't recognise that bit of cloth, and I don't know how it would have got there.'

'It seemed to be hidden pretty deliberately. What would you say the odds were of a mobile phone accidentally landing in a piece of cloth, somehow wrapping itself up and being dropped behind a radiator of its own accord?'

'*Is* there any evidence that this is my client's phone, or are you merely speculating?' Brian asks.

McKenna ignores him. 'Amy, do you recognise the mobile number 07700 900494?'

I swallow. 'Yes. It's my number.'

'We called that number after retrieving the phone, and it showed as a missed call on the phone we retrieved. It was on Do Not Disturb mode, which meant it went straight through to answerphone and wouldn't vibrate if a text message or email came through. So there's no way anyone would have heard it ringing or vibrating behind the radiator — because it wasn't. Do you think that's the sort of thing someone might do if they were deliberately trying to hide it?'

'I... I don't know,' I say.

'But it is your mobile phone, yes?'

'I don't know. If you say so.'

I try to work out what the hell's going on. The enormity of it is clear, but it makes no sense. I desperately try to think back to when I last saw my phone. It didn't seem particularly relevant before, but now I realise everything could hinge on it. My future could depend on it.

'We haven't been able to do a full analysis on it yet, Amy, but forensics told us it looks as though someone's tried to clean it. There are microscopic traces of blood on the phone. Do you know whose they might be?'

I feel my throat starting to close up. This can't be happening.

'Did you cut yourself recently? That might explain it.'

I shake my head. I can't speak.

McKenna leans forward. 'Amy, this isn't starting to look particularly good, is it? I know you're not keen on speaking with us, but I really do think it might be in your best interests to tell us exactly what happened this morning.'

20

I'm desperately trying to work out what's going on here. I'm convinced that sooner or later I'm going to wake up and find out it was all a dream. It has to be. There's no other option.

You hear these stories about people doing things in their sleep, or when they've blanked out. But that can't be the case. It didn't happen while I was asleep — I was sitting out in the garden all morning, reading my book. I remember every minute of it. Don't I?

I'd certainly remember putting my book down, getting in my car, driving to Roger's house and murdering him. Besides which, I remember realising when I got up on Friday morning that I couldn't find my phone and thought I must have left it at work. That was a whole twenty-four hours before Roger died. I planned to have a look when I got there, but totally forgot.

I was pretty sure I plugged my phone in to charge in the kitchen on Thursday night. I can't be certain, though. It's just routine. If I have my phone on me when I'm going up to bed, I plug it in to charge in the kitchen overnight. I always have. We all do.

I always said when the boys got their first iPad that it'd be totally locked down with parental controls and wouldn't go anywhere near their bedrooms at night. They'd have to leave it downstairs. I didn't want them playing on it all night or having to check it and play on it the second they woke up.

So maybe I did leave my phone at work on Thursday. But I certainly didn't pick it up on Friday, so how the hell did it manage to get back home, then to Roger's house and back on Saturday morning? None of it makes any sense.

My body feels like it's shutting down. There's nothing I can do. Every direction I turn, there seems to be something else that's determined to see me go down for murder. A murder I didn't commit.

At first I thought there must have been some huge mistake. Roger's neighbour was clearly senile or thought he saw something he didn't. I can kind of see why they would have arrested me based on that. But that should have been where it all ended.

There's a knock on my cell door and it opens. The police officer tells me Brian wants to meet with me in one of the consultation rooms. I tell her to send him into my cell. I'm fed up of being dragged from pillar to post.

Brian's head pokes round the door. 'It really would be best if you came with me,' he says.

I let out a huge sigh, get to my feet and follow them.

Once we're in the consultation room, Brian coughs slightly before speaking.

'Sorry about that. I never fully trust conversations in cells — they have a camera and microphone in there, you know. They say it's to check on your safety, but you can never be too sure. At times like this it's best to keep our cards close to our chest. You don't see the police letting you in on what they know.'

I can't work Brian out. Sometimes he says things like this which make me think he's on my side, and at others I wonder if he thinks I've actually done this and just wants to get shot of me. Looking at it totally impartially, I'm not sure if I'd want to represent me in court right now. But that doesn't change the fact that I'm entirely innocent and I *have* to walk free. I need to get out of here.

'I just wanted a quick debrief with you after the last interview. I've been having a look through everything and trying to work out where we go from here. I realise you're pleading your innocence, and I respect that. I really do. But my job is to look at this in purely black and white terms, from the point of view of the police, CPS and the courts. I represent you, of course, but I need to be able to see things from their side and get an idea of where things might be heading. Sometimes damage limitation is the best we can hope for.'

'But I haven't done anything,' I plead. 'There's no damage to limit. I didn't do anything.'

'I'll be honest with you,' he says, 'and this probably isn't what you want to hear, but that's actually kind of irrelevant. The weight of evidence is growing. If it comes back that the blood on that phone is Roger's, it's Good-night Vienna.' He looks at me for a few moments, trying to suss me out. 'Do you think it'll come back saying it's Roger's?'

I close my eyes. I want to tell him I don't know, but deep down I do. I know it's going to be his.

'Brian, I didn't kill Roger. I wasn't there. I was at home. I don't know what happened to my phone or where it went, but I promise you I had nothing to do with any of this. I know nothing about it. Everything they tell me is totally new to me.'

Brian sits back in his chair and exhales heavily. 'Okay. Let's look at this step by step. Around nine o'clock this morning, someone knocks on your father-in-law's door and is let into the house. Presumably he knew them or was expecting them. A minute or so later he's beaten to death in his own kitchen, with no real sign of a struggle. A neighbour then sees someone leave, who he identifies as you. The police have traced your mobile phone's move-ments as being identical to this. That phone then heads back to your house and is found hidden there later in the day, with traces of blood on it. Meanwhile, you have no alibi or evidence to place you elsewhere.'

I go to protest, but Brian raises his hand to silence me. 'I'm just telling you how it is,' he explains. 'Those are the facts. I've inferred no guilt — I've merely stated the truths of what happened. And yes, you're absolutely right, it does make you sound incredibly guilty and I can see exactly why you wanted to object to it as I was saying it. And that's exactly my point. The evidence is almost over-whelming. Almost.'

I lean forward and look at him. 'Go on,' I say.

'Well, if we can shed some doubt on their evidence or methodology, or introduce a possibility which negates the evidence they've collected so far, we might be in with a chance.' He swallows and leans forward to meet my eyes. 'But I need to ask you something very directly. You'll have to forgive me for treading over old ground, and I know you've plead your innocence continually, but I've been doing this job a long time and I like to think I'm a pretty good judge of character.'

'Ask me,' I say, knowing what he's going to say before he says it.

Brian clears his throat gently. 'Amy, did you kill Roger Walker?'

'No,' I reply, as clearly and confidently as I can.

'Do you know who did?'

'No.'

'Were you at or near the scene?'

'No. Everything I've told you is true.'

He looks at me for a moment, then nods slowly. 'Alright,' he says, leaning back and sorting through his papers. 'Then it looks like you and I have some work to do.'

21

For the first time since my arrest, I'm starting to feel at least slightly hopeful.

'As I see it,' Brian says, 'the evidence is starting to look pretty overwhelming on face value. And this is where certain laws of logic start to come into play. Are you familiar with confirmation bias?'

I shake my head.

'As human beings, we're conditioned to look for patterns. We have our preexisting and predetermined beliefs, and we seek information that confirms those biases. It's something the police have to be extremely careful about. The surer and surer they are that you're guilty, the more they'll interpret evidence as being an assumption of that guilt, and will tend to overlook anything which might be evidence of your innocence.'

'Right,' I say. I think I'm starting to see what he means, but I don't know how this is going to help me.

'The CPS and the courts will be looking at this afresh, mind. They don't know you or the police officers. They're impartial and won't be susceptible to confirmation bias. That goes in our favour somewhat, but it does mean we'll need evidence that either proves our case or sheds doubt on what the police are alleging. Are you familiar with the term "beyond reasonable doubt"?'

I nod. 'I think so.'

'It's the measure juries adhere to when they're being asked to judge the defendant's guilt or innocence. They can't find someone guilty just because they think they did it, or because there's more evidence on one side than the other. They have to be certain *beyond reasonable doubt* that the defendant committed the crime. And that's where the burden of proof lies far more heavily on the prosecution, you see?'

The look on my face tells Brian he's probably starting to lose me a bit. 'Look at it this way,' he says. 'We don't need to *beat* their evidence as such. We don't need more evidence than them. We don't even need better evidence than them. We just need to be able to introduce that shred of doubt into the jury's minds, so that the crucial element of reasonable doubt exists. Do you follow?'

I nod. I do follow.

'So the prosecution not only have to provide enough watertight evidence to convict, but they have to ensure that there's absolutely no doubt in the jury's mind. Their job is a lot harder than ours. And it has to be for the system to be fair. If you're innocent, there'll always be a way to introduce reasonable doubt. And that's what we now have to look for.'

'But how?' I ask. 'There's nothing. I don't even have an alibi.'

'Ah, but that would be evidence in your favour. Let's assume for now we don't have that and are focusing on introducing reasonable doubt. In England and Wales you can only be guilty or not guilty. If we were playing this little game in Scotland, we'd be shooting for a "not proven" verdict. But they can keep that little oddity north of the border as far as I'm concerned. Our laws mean we can very reasonably aim for not guilty.

'There are two main ways we can do this,' he says. 'We can either introduce an element of doubt with regards to the prosecution's evidence or methodology, which obviously they're not keen on. That has to be handled very carefully. Blindly accusing the police of malpractice tends not to go down too well in court. The other is to introduce some possibility which could at best negate the evidence they've collected, and at worst remain open and impossible to be disproved by the prosecution.'

'I… I'm not sure what you mean,' I say.

Brian exhales. 'Look, this is all stuff a barrister and legal team would go through. My job will end long before then, but I keep a close eye on what happens that side of the wall. Ponder this for a moment, if you will. The absolute, irrefutable facts are that your mobile phone travelled from the vicinity of your house, to Roger's house and back to the vicinity of your house around the time of the murder. They can prove that. They can't prove you were with it. It's not up to us to *prove* you weren't, but to at least introduce reasonable doubt that you might not have been.'

I nod slowly.

'You admit you're careless with your phone, yes? That you lose it quite often. Then all we need to do is introduce the possibility that someone else took your phone with them, then returned it to your house, and that particular piece of evidence is worthless.'

'Yes, but who? There isn't anyone.'

'Oh, I'm sure there are plenty of people. Who has access to your house?'

'No-one really,' I say. 'Our next-door neighbours down the lane have a key. So did Roger. And Brendan, of course.'

'I see,' Brian says.

'And the neighbours. They're in their mid-eighties, for crying out loud. They can barely get as far as their front gate.'

'Mmmm,' Brian says. The inference in this noise is crystal clear to me.

'No. No. Brendan was at the football with the boys. They were both there with him, and there'd be dozens of other people there too who'd be witnesses or alibis or whatever you want to call them.'

'All we need to do is introduce the possibility, Amy,' Brian says.

'No. It's not a possibility. There'll be witnesses. He was there with the boys. There's no way he did anything. And anyway, Roger's neighbour reckons he saw me there. My husband and I don't exactly look alike.'

'No, but from that distance he could have been mistaken. A wig and some carefully chosen clothes can do a lot. You'd be amazed what the brain fills in.'

'He's six foot four!' I yell. 'He's almost eight inches taller than me, and built like a rugby player.'

Brian leans forward slowly.

'Amy, you didn't kill your father-in-law, right?'

I nod. 'Correct.'

'Well somebody did. And that person knew you. They had access to your house. They knew Roger. And Roger knew them. I think it's about time you started asking yourself some uncomfortable questions.'

22

Simon Robinson knocked at the door of 14 Park View Road and waited for a response. Ten seconds later, it came.

'Simon, hi,' Brendan said as he opened the door. 'Thanks so much for coming, especially on a Sunday.'

'No problem,' Simon replied. 'It's my pleasure.'

'Just, y'know — trying to discuss work stuff with the wife and kids around…'

'Totally agree. Best to do it while they're all out, eh?'

Brendan smiled and ushered Simon through to the kitchen.

'Nice place,' Simon said. 'Gorgeous kitchen.'

'Thanks. It's only been in about six months, but we're really pleased with it.'

Simon looked around. It wasn't the biggest kitchen

he'd ever seen, but it was smartly designed and made the most of the space that was there.

'You gadget fans too?' he said, gesturing towards the tangle of cables in one corner of the work surface.

'Something like that. That's the Central Charging Hotel. For some reason everything gets plugged in there at night. Phones, kids' iPad, the lot. I don't know how anyone keeps track of what's what.'

'They've got wireless charging on the new ones, apparently. But you still need to plug the charging pad into the wall and have your phone within inches of it anyway, so I don't see how that's any major improvement.'

'No, but I bet you any money we'll have six by the end of the year.'

Simon let out a small chuckle. 'So,' he said, sitting down at the small table. 'Business good?'

Brendan laughed. 'You tell me. You're the accountant.'

Simon gave him his best smile. 'All looks good to me.'

'Good. Yeah. It feels good, too, you know? I mean, I always said it wouldn't be my sort of thing taking over the company, but I think I'm really starting to enjoy it. It's going well.'

Simon smiled again. He never had been sure quite what to make of Brendan. Things had been far more straightforward with his old man. Roger'd had a clear direction for the business. He'd been running it for years. It had become second nature to him. With Brendan, things were different.

Brendan seemed far more unsure than his father had. At first, anyway. But over the past year or so Simon had watched him grow in confidence. He liked to think that perhaps he'd had a part to play in that. Maybe they'd both grown together; Simon had been a newly qualified accountant when he'd been hired by Morris & Co.

David Morris, the owner of the accountancy firm, had seen it as a sign of the times, he said. He'd been thinking of taking a step back at the same time as his old friend Roger, with new blood coming through the ranks in both companies. With a little bit of persuasion from Simon, the company was added to his portfolio of clients.

'I know the year-end stuff isn't due for a while yet,' Brendan said, placing two mugs of tea on the table and sitting down, 'but I wanted to run a couple of ideas past you. One, mainly.'

'Alright. Shoot.'

'Okay. So. My dad's been great, as you know. He built the company up from scratch and left it in a good state for me to take over. He was faultless through the transition, too. Really supportive, everything. It's just... It's been three years, you know? Two since Dad stopped having any real input. I know he's been putting into a pension scheme for years, and he's hardly short of money. And I just think it might be time to ask him to cut the reins completely. If you see what I mean.'

'You want to buy out his shares?' Simon asked.

'I think so, yeah. I mean, it makes sense. I've got ideas for the company. It'll change. It won't be the same as the company Dad built up and I wouldn't want him to feel conflicted by being a shareholder but not agreeing to my ideas.'

'No, but you do have the controlling stake,' Simon said. 'Your dad only owns twenty-five percent.'

'I know. But that twenty-five percent gave him a dividend of over thirty grand last year. Without having done any work for the past two. Or having run the company for the last three.'

Simon cocked his head and raised his eyebrows. 'Well, I can see your point. It's a lot of money to pay out each year.'

'Especially when it could be going to us. To the kids,' Brendan added.

'Sure. Have you spoken to him about it?'

Brendan sighed and looked away for a moment. 'No. No, I haven't. You know what he's like. I don't think he'd take it in the spirit it was meant. He's not the sort of person who takes suggestions off people, you know? Especially not from me, anyway.'

Simon smiled. Roger Walker had always been headstrong, but in a good way. He was focused, organised and dedicated.

Brendan continued. 'He's the sort of person who does things when he thinks they were his own idea. That's why I thought, maybe, someone else might be able to plant the seed in his mind.'

'Me?' Simon asked.

'I was thinking more David. He and Dad go back years.'

'Couldn't you plant the seed yourself?'

Brendan shook his head. 'He'd see right through that. He's too canny. David seems to be the only person Dad ever listens to. I'm sure if the suggestion came from him, he'd definitely consider it.'

'Well, you never know, I guess,' Simon said, sitting back in his chair, feeling the hard wooden frame against his back. 'Have you spoken to Amy about it?'

'Not yet. I was planning to. But I wanted to put out a couple of feelers first. See if you think it might be doable.'

'Everything's doable. Business is just numbers on a spreadsheet. Budge a few over into another column and everything looks completely different.'

Brendan nodded. Simon could tell he was beginning to see the possibilities.

'So how would you suggest we approach it?' Brendan asked.

The royal we. 'I guess I could speak to David. Maybe mention that business is doing well and that you're looking to expand. Suggest that perhaps cutting free of the old ties might be in everyone's best interests.'

'Great. Thanks. I'd really appreciate that. I just think it'd be best for everyone, you know?'

'Sure. No problem.'

'I owe you one, Simon. Big time.'

Simon took a sip of his tea and smiled. 'Don't worry. I'll think of something.'

23

I'm allowed a phone call. According to Brian, now I've been interviewed a few times and they've completed the search at my house, they no longer consider it a risk for me to phone someone.

I'm not sure what risk they think I pose, but Brian says they would be worried I might try to get a message out to an accomplice of some sort. It all sounds so bizarre, so far removed from my normal, everyday life.

I've even started to question myself, begun to wonder if perhaps I *could* have done it. After all, the evidence seems so overwhelming. But I know I didn't. I can't have done. I don't have a history of mental illness or forgetfulness. I don't black out or sleepwalk. Not at nine o'clock in the morning, when I know damn well I was sitting in my back garden.

Brian said it wouldn't be wise to ask if I could call

Brendan. After all, I'm being questioned on suspicion of murdering his father. The fact he's my husband doesn't actually matter at the moment. Not to the police, anyway.

It sort of makes sense from the police's point of view, but seems incredibly unfair to me. All I want to do is tell my husband I had nothing to do with all of this. His dad's dead, and I just want to be there for him, to hold him and to tell him everything's going to be okay. Instead, I'm sitting in a jail cell, suspected of having killed him myself.

But I think I've got a way round it.

I ask if I can make my phone call, and I'm taken out of my cell and back to the custody desk where I was booked in earlier today.

The custody sergeant asks who I want to call. He doesn't seem as polite or humane as the one who was here earlier. In fact, he doesn't appear to be particularly bothered by my presence at all. It's almost as if I'm getting in the way, cluttering up the place.

'I'd like to call my mum, please,' I say.

He asks me for the number, and I give it to him. Moments later, we're connected.

'Mum? It's me,' I manage to say, before I give way to uncontrollable sobbing.

In that moment, just hearing my mum's voice on the line, it all comes out. I've been managing to hold it together up until now, hoping they'd very quickly realise what a huge mistake this all is, but the second I speak to my mum I become a little girl again.

'It's okay,' Mum says, eventually. 'We'll get this all sorted out.' There's a pause. 'Amy, what happened?'

'I don't know, Mum. I wasn't there. I promise you. I was at home all morning. I know nothing about any of this, I swear. I have no idea what's going on. The police keep interviewing me and showing me new stuff and asking me about things and making out like I had something to do with it. They keep coming up with new things that seem to prove I did it, but I didn't!'

'Amy, it's okay. Just stay calm. It'll all be over soon, I'm sure. They're probably just doing their job. Are they looking after you okay? Do you need anything?'

I can tell by Mum's voice that she hasn't been made privy to any of the so-called evidence the police have found. I wonder if they've told anyone.

'No. It's fine. How is everyone?' I ask, hoping Mum reads between the lines.

'The boys are alright. Missing their mum, of course, but I told them you'll be home soon.'

I try to fight back the tears as Mum says this. I dearly hope she's right.

'Brendan's in shock, as you can imagine,' Mum says. 'He doesn't know which way to turn.'

I can't even imagine how he must be feeling. But I know Brendan. Mum's right — he has no-one. Being an only child, and with both parents now gone, the only place he'd have left to turn is to my mum. They've always got on so well, I know he'd have no qualms about going to her in a situation like this.

'Is he there?' I ask, trying to make the question sound perfectly normal, so as not to rouse the suspicion of the custody sergeant. To be honest, I could probably stand here constructing a nail bomb and he wouldn't even raise an eyebrow.

'He's in the front room. I'm in the kitchen.'

Mum's tone is very matter-of-fact, as if the underlying message is that it wouldn't be a great idea to talk to him. But this is my only chance. If this ends up in a charge and going to trial, it might be the last opportunity I get to speak to Brendan. If he believes that the police are saying, then...

'Can I speak to him please? Just quickly.'

I hear Mum sigh. 'I really don't think that's a good idea, Amy. Not considering the circumstances.'

'Please, Mum,' I say, in the tone of voice I reserve only for when I really mean it. Again, I feel like a little girl, begging my mum for a biscuit, knowing it's only half an hour until dinner time. 'Please.'

Mum's silent for a moment. 'I'll ask him,' she says.

There's a period of quiet, as Mum presumably goes into the living room to speak to Brendan. I clench my fists, hoping the custody sergeant isn't about to suddenly realise I exist and tell me my time's up.

Then I hear a voice on the line. One it seems as

though I haven't heard for years, even though it's barely been hours.

'Amy,' Brendan says. I can't pick up much from the tone, and I can't even begin to imagine what's going through his mind right now.

'Hi,' I say, trying desperately to hold onto my voice. 'I just wanted to say this is all a huge mistake. All of it. I didn't do anything. You have to believe me.'

The pause is longer than I'm comfortable with. 'Okay.'

'What do you mean "okay"?' I ask. 'You have to believe me. I wasn't there. I was at home all morning. Why the hell would I want to do something like that? It makes no sense.'

'Amy, I don't know what to think,' Brendan says. He sounds like a broken man. 'I've gone from family man to bereaved son with a wife in prison, all in the space of a couple of hours. What do you want me to say?'

I blink and try to push back the tears.

'I want you to say you believe me.'

That uncomfortable silence again.

'You do believe me, don't you?'

'Amy, they found your phone in the house. Hidden. With blood on it. They... they found the text messages.'

This hits me right in the gut, like a sucker punch. They've been telling Brendan everything. 'They told you?'

I hear Brendan swallow. 'They've been keeping me updated with developments. I asked them to. There was a woman here earlier. A family liaison officer. I told her I wanted to know what was going on as it happened.'

I go to say his name, but manage to stop myself just in time.

'You have to believe me. I had nothing to do with this. Someone's… someone's setting me up.'

'What?' Brendan says, his voice verging on incredulity. 'Why the hell would anyone want to do that?'

I swallow. 'I don't know. But there's no other possibility. Someone put that phone there. Someone sent those texts from it.'

I leave that hanging in the air. I think back to what Brian told me, the unspoken insinuation that Brendan could be involved.

I wait for his reply, but none comes.

The next sound I hear is the click of Brendan hanging up the phone.

24

Amy snuggled into Lewis as the film took another dramatic turn. She watched through her fingers as Ryan Phillippe's character was murdered on the balcony, only for the police to discover no sign of either killer or victim.

The film had been Lewis's suggestion. One he'd seen at the cinema when it came out last year. It wasn't Amy's sort of thing, but she didn't really fancy the idea of arguing with him.

'Good, yeah?' Lewis grunted. He stank of cigarettes and cheap booze, even though it was barely four o'clock in the afternoon.

His and Greg's flat had become a shrine to alcohol, parties and drugs ever since they'd moved in a few months earlier. Lewis had always been a bit of a livewire, but having his own space and personal freedom had only added tinder to those sparks.

At just fifteen, Amy was both impressed by her boyfriend's own flat but also slightly disgusted at the way he and Greg lived. She always had the impression Greg kept Lewis reined in somewhat, and wondered what Lewis would be like if he lived on his own. She didn't suppose he'd last five minutes. She was just pleased he hadn't asked her to move in with him. She was far too fond of her creature comforts to make that move. She knew she had it easy living at home with her mum.

'You scared?' he asked, smirking slightly.

'No,' she replied, not entirely convincingly.

'Yeah you are. Shitting yourself.'

'I'm not. I'm just cuddling you, that's all.'

Lewis shuffled slightly and kissed her on the top of her head. 'You sure that's all?'

She could smell the booze and fags wafting down on his breath again. 'Yeah, pretty sure,' she replied.

Lewis placed a hand on her breast. 'Cos I could think of one or two other things we could throw into the mix,' he said.

Amy smiled and adjusted her body. 'I'm cool with a cuddle. Anyway, I'm enjoying the film.'

Lewis laughed. 'No you're not.'

'I am.'

'You're not. I know you. You hate this sort of stuff.'

Why did you suggest we watch it then? Amy wanted to ask, but didn't. She didn't see any wisdom in deliberately antagonising him.

'I don't. I like some of it. I like this one.'

'What's it called then?'

Amy flicked her eyes down to the floor, hoping to catch a glimpse of the title on the VHS cassette box.

'Oi, no cheating. Come on. What's it called?'

She placed her head back on his chest. 'It doesn't matter what it's called. I'm enjoying it. Alright?'

'Alright,' Lewis replied.

They watched the film in silence for a few seconds longer before Lewis spoke again.

'I know what you did last summer.'

Amy's heart jumped. 'What?' she said, her throat dry and her voice raspy.

'That's what the film's called. *I Know What You Did Last Summer*. That's the title.'

Amy swallowed and forced a smile. 'Oh. Yeah. I remember now.'

'She's pretty fit, don't you think?'

Amy tried not to give him the reaction he wanted. 'Who?'

'The one playing Helen.'

'She's alright I guess.'

'I'd give her one.'

Amy didn't respond. She knew he was only doing it to try and get a rise out of her. She didn't know why he did these things. Maybe he wanted her to show her dedication for him — as if she was going to be jealous at the super-realistic prospect of Sarah Michelle Gellar swooping in and stealing her pigeon-chested stick insect of a boyfriend from her. Unless Sarah Michelle Gellar had a penchant for unkempt greasy hair and the faint smell of weed, Amy presumed her relationship was pretty safe.

Not that she'd be particularly bothered if someone did take him off her hands. It would be a whole lot easier than dumping him. Sure, he had his good moments — and it was a bonus having an older boyfriend with his own car and flat — but for the most part he was a prick.

'Shame she's not here, though,' he said, putting his hand between her legs. 'I suppose you'll just have to do instead.'

Amy moved his hand away. 'I'm watching the film.'

'You can watch at the same time,' he said, putting his hand back. 'Don't mind me.'

'Later.'

'Yeah, later as well if you want. Come on, get them off.'

'I don't want to. Let's do it later.'

Lewis sat up. 'Fuck's wrong with you? When have you ever turned down a shag?'

Again, Amy chose not to rise to the bait. She'd learned long ago just to let his snide comments wash over her, but there was still no way in hell she was going to let him force himself on her. She had some dignity.

'I'm not turning you down. I just said later. Let's watch the film for now.'

Lewis picked up the remote control, switched off the TV and threw the remote at the mirror over the mantle piece, a spider's web pattern appearing across the cracked glass.

'Fuck the film. Film's off. Gone. Now come on. Suck my cock.'

'No. I don't want to.'

'What do you mean you don't fucking want to? You're my girlfriend. It's what you're meant to do.'

'It's not all I'm here for, Lewis. I am meant to have other uses too.'

Lewis looked at her for a moment, then laughed. 'Fuck off. Seriously, just fuck off.'

Amy looked back, trying to work out whether he was serious or not.

'Go on. Get the fuck out. Fucking timewaster.'

Amy swallowed hard, and tried to bite her tongue. As she put her shoes on and got to the door, Lewis called from behind her.

'Same time tomorrow, yeah?'

25

'Is Lewis in?' Amy asked, trying to hold her stomach as she experienced the smell emanating from the flat.

Greg shook his head. 'Not at the moment, no. Come in if you want.'

'It's alright. Do you know when he's going to be back?'

'I dunno. You tried calling him?'

'Yeah. No reply.'

Greg gave her a pitiful smile. 'Come on, come in.'

Amy stepped inside the flat and watched as Greg closed the door.

'What's happened this time?' Greg asked, as he led her through to the living room area.

'Christ knows. The usual. We were watching a film, he got all arsey 'cos I wouldn't... Well, you know.'

Greg let out a small laugh. 'Sounds about right. He'll never change. You know that.'

Amy raised her eyebrows slightly and let out a sigh. 'Yeah. I know. But you still hope, you know. I mean, he's not all bad. And now I feel terrible for being like that with him. I can see why he got annoyed.'

Greg sat down on the sofa. 'Really? I can't.'

'You can't?'

'No. If you didn't want to do stuff, you didn't want to do stuff. He's got no right to demand anything. It's your body, isn't it?'

Amy thought about this for a moment. 'I guess so. But I'm his girlfriend. I should be willing to... you know.'

Greg shrugged. 'If you don't want to, you don't want to. Would you try and make him do something he didn't want to do?'

'I guess not.'

'Exactly.'

Amy cocked her head slightly and looked at him. 'Why are you saying this, though? You're his best mate.'

Greg laughed. 'I might be his best mate, but he's not mine. What do you think it's like trying to live with the bloke? Nah, I mean he's alright, but he's a bit of a dick sometimes.'

Amy laughed too. 'That just about sums it up, yeah. But I do love him, you know?'

Greg smiled. 'I know.'

Amy sat in silence for a moment. She felt comfortable

here, but she still couldn't shake those feelings in her mind.

'Did he say anything to you?' she asked. 'After the other night, I mean.'

'Like what?'

Amy shuffled awkwardly. 'I dunno. Like, did he tell you what happened, or make any sort of comment or anything?'

Greg shook his head. 'Not that I can remember. You know what he's like. He keeps himself to himself with stuff like that. Anyway, we're just flatmates. We're blokes. We don't sit around talking about our feelings.'

Amy sighed. 'Maybe it might help him.'

Greg looked at her for a moment. 'Maybe.'

'You must just think I'm young and stupid,' Amy said.

'Not especially, no.'

'It's different for him, I suppose. He's had other girl-friends. He's got his own flat. A job. But that doesn't mean I'm just some silly little girl.'

Greg leaned forward and put his hand on Amy's shoulder. 'Hey. No-one ever said any of this stuff. No-one thinks that about you.'

'I bet Lewis does.'

'I don't think he does,' Greg replied. 'And I certainly don't.'

Amy looked at him. It was a bizarre set of circum-stances. Lewis was the person she should be able to go to when she wanted to explain her feelings, or to get some sort of comfort and support. Yet, more often than not, it tended to be Greg who was there for her.

There'd never been any suggestion of anything going on between the two of them, of course. Definitely not. If Lewis even had a hint of an idea about anything like that, he'd hit the roof.

She couldn't get over how different Lewis and Greg were. They'd been friends since primary school, but they were like chalk and cheese. The education system and school culture usually end up inadvertently dividing kids into cliques. There's the cool kids, the footballers, the geeks, the beauty queens, the fighters — the list went on. But, somehow, two kids like Lewis and Greg ended up sticking together.

Greg always seemed far more sensitive than Lewis, but not in the conventional way. It was more a case of worrying about things unnecessarily. Even an unexpected knock at the door would make Greg jump and yelp like a kicked puppy.

Once, when Greg wasn't there, Lewis told Amy that Greg's mother had been killed when he was nine years old. She'd taken the two of them out to a lake for the day, and the boys had been playing. He didn't go into details, but said Greg's mum was attacked by a man. He hit her over the head with a log or a tree branch and killed her instantly. Amy hadn't wanted to go into the details or ask too many questions, but ever since then she'd looked at Greg with a newfound admiration and sympathy.

Amy had always been floating somewhere between 'geek' and 'lost child'. Her parents had split up when she was eleven — a crucial time in her life. Just when she was starting to become a woman, and when she'd most needed the support of her parents, they'd been more preoccupied with bickering and trying to get one over on each other.

She was a bright girl — always had been — and even at the age of fifteen she was acutely aware that she was probably attracted to Lewis because he was a strong character, a man who knew what he wanted at all times. She might not agree with him most of the time, but that didn't matter. There was direction, even if that direction was a little unclear to her at times.

Often, that came across as being controlling. Things always had to be done his way. If he wanted to go out to see a film, they were going out to see a film. If he wanted to stay at home and smoke, they were going to stay at home and smoke.

But Amy really didn't mind that. It was refreshing and novel not to have to decide everything for herself, to be able to acquiesce to someone else every once in a while.

'Do you think I'm daft for staying with him?' Amy asked.

Greg took a deep breath and cocked his head. 'No, I don't think I'd say that. You've got to do what you've got to do, haven't you? If you love him, you're going to want to stay with him. It's not up to anyone else to tell you what to do.'

Amy smiled. Greg never said a bad word against anyone. He was always so… diplomatic. That was the word. Diplomatic. She didn't know anyone who disliked Greg, mainly because he always seemed to go so far out of his way to make sure he didn't offend or upset anybody.

It was reassuring to know that there were people out there who really cared — people who really did have your back.

26

I think I managed to get some sleep. I don't how how much, but it wasn't a lot. If I wasn't physically lying awake I was tossing and turning. By the time I'd managed to relax my mind and stop torturing myself about everything, I was struggling to get comfortable on the horrendous blue plastic mattress in my cell.

Every time I nodded off there'd be a bang, or a clattering of a cell door, or someone shouting and screaming somewhere along the corridor.

I don't know how much more of this I can take. I shouldn't be here. Even the food's horrendous and devoid of flavour. They brought me breakfast about an hour ago. I couldn't even work out what half of it was meant to be. If I stay here much longer I'm likely to starve to death.

Before I can worry about that too much, my cell door opens and I'm told the police want to interview me again. I don't know why they couldn't just do all this in one interview. Why do they need to keep dragging me in every time they think they've turned a corner or want to ask me something else? I'm sure they've got their reasons, but I can't think of any that don't involve them slowly trying to break me and get me to admit to killing Roger.

But I won't. I'll never do that. I'm absolutely determined not to go down for this.

DI McKenna looks like she's had about as much sleep as I have. I can't imagine it's much fun for detectives when they have to stay up all night working on a big case, but I don't exactly have much sympathy with her right now. She seems hell-bent on assuming I killed Roger, and nothing I say is going to convince her otherwise. All it does is give her further fuel to twist my words and make me sound guilty.

She does her usual interview preamble and then gets down to business. I get the feeling she enjoys interviews. She must get some sort of kick out of it, like the courtroom lawyer who revels in holding back a key piece of information until the defendant has backed themselves into a corner, ready for that final pummelling.

'Amy, we should just tell you before we begin that we've been given permission to extend your detention in custody by a further twelve hours.'

I say nothing, but inside I'm crying. Brian had told me they could and probably would extend the twenty-four-hour custody clock, but I'd always hoped it would be over and done with long before then.

'Amy, in your last couple of interviews you told us you didn't go to Roger Walker's house yesterday morning, is that correct?'

'Yes,' I say. I've already told Brian I'm not interested in his advice on no-commenting my way through interviews. I've got a right to give my side of the story, and if I can tell them the truth there's no way I can go down for this. The truth has to win out. Doesn't it?

'And do you still assert that's the case?'

'Yes. I do. I was at home all morning. The first time I left the house was in the back of a police car.'

'What about your car?' McKenna asks.

'What about it?'

'Was anyone driving it yesterday morning?'

I shake my head. 'No. The only people who drive the cars are me and Brendan, and Brendan was at the football in the other one.'

McKenna turns her laptop round and shows me a picture on the screen.

'Can you tell me whose car this is please, Amy?'

I stare at the picture. It looks like a CCTV still. It's zoomed in on a car, a Ford Fiesta, which bears the number plate FO17 UTA.

'It looks like mine,' I say.

'Is it yours? Is that your registration number?' McKenna asks.

I look at it again. 'Yeah.'

'That picture is from a CCTV camera on the high street. It's timestamped at 8.56 yesterday morning. The car's heading west, roughly in the direction of Roger Walker's house. Do you remember why?'

I swallow. 'No. Well no, it can't be. The car was on the drive all morning.'

'Are you sure?' McKenna asks.

'Yeah. Brendan was out, and I was in. No-one has access to it.'

'So you don't think someone could have taken it?'

I look at her. 'If you think I'm going to try and claim someone must have taken my car so I can wriggle out of this, you're very much mistaken. No, no one could have taken my car. That's the truth. But that still doesn't change the fact that it wasn't me.'

McKenna looks at me for a moment, then nods slowly. She brings up another picture on the laptop screen.

'There was another active camera on the high street. This one was facing in the other direction, so we can see the front of the car. Have a look, Amy. If we zoom in closer the picture quality suffers a bit, but let me tell you what I see. That looks very much to me like a young woman, perhaps in her late thirties, with long blonde hair. Do you agree?'

I swallow again. 'Well, yes.'

'It looks a lot like you, doesn't it Amy?'

I stutter for a moment. 'Yes.'

'And that's because it is you, isn't it Amy?'

'No.'

'You were driving down the high street yesterday morning, in your car, in the direction of your father-in-law's house, only minutes before he was murdered.'

'No.'

McKenna brings up two further pictures.

'These images were taken thirteen minutes later. Your car, with you driving it, heading back in the opposite direction. Where did you go, Amy?'

I start to shake, my voice catching in my throat.

'No... nowhere. I didn't go anywhere. That isn't me. It can't be me.'

'It's your car, Amy. And the person driving it looks a lot like you. In between these photos being taken, you were seen at Roger's house, coming out and getting into this car. Your mobile phone records back this up to the second.'

I'm stunned into silence.

'Do you want to say anything, Amy?' McKenna asks.

I blink and shake my head.

'Okay. We analysed the blood spatters on your mobile phone. The one we found hidden down the back of your downstairs bathroom radiator. The analysis indicates that blood is Roger's. Do you have anything to say about that?'

I can feel my heartbeat pounding in my eardrums, my

chest hammering. This can't be happening. None of it makes any sense.

'How did your father-in-law's blood get on your phone, Amy?'

I don't answer. I can't speak. I barely hear the words she's saying to me. All I can hear is my entire world crashing down around me. I've nowhere to go, nowhere to turn. I'm completely lost.

'Amy, we found the hammer.'

I close my eyes, hoping that when I open them again this will have all gone away.

'It was in the woodland next to your house, maybe eight feet or so from the boundary of your property. Did you throw it there when you got back from Roger's?'

There's nothing I can say. Nothing will make this better. Nothing will convince them I'm innocent.

'Amy, the hammer has blood and fragments of tissue on it. They haven't been analysed yet, but we have no reason to believe they're not Roger's. Do you want to say anything?'

I don't.

McKenna is silent for a few moments. 'Did you and Roger fall out, Amy?'

'No. We've always got on really well. This is what I mean — I had no reason to kill him. Why would I do that?'

McKenna looks at her colleague, then down at the desk and finally back at me. 'When somebody is killed, we try to retrace their steps in their final days. We know from Roger's diary that he met with David Morris the day before he died. Do you know Mr Morris?'

'Uh, yeah. He's the accountant. Well, he runs Morris & Co, the accountancy firm we use. He's been a friend of Roger's for years.'

McKenna nods. 'Do you know what was discussed at the meeting?'

I shrug. 'No, I wasn't there.'

'We spoke to David. The meeting concerned some financial irregularities they'd discovered in the company. David went to Roger as his oldest friend and as a share-holder to let him know what he'd found.'

My eyes narrow. 'Irregularities? What irregularities?'

'Apparently there were false invoices being created and submitted for suppliers who didn't exist. These invoices were then being paid out. Who's in charge of invoicing at the company, Amy?'

'I am,' I say quietly.

'They haven't quite managed to go through every-thing yet, but they estimate around £65,000 was stolen from the company using these false invoices.'

'But that's not possible,' I say. 'I enter all the invoices myself. I know all our regular suppliers.'

'Who else has access to the system?' McKenna asks.

'No-one. I enter them into our bookkeeping package, then the accountant goes in at the end of the year and grabs the data for the year end accounts.'

Brian speaks up. 'Have you managed to trace where this money went, Detective Inspector? And can you link it with my client?'

McKenna smiles. 'We're working on that.' She watches me for a few moments. 'David told Roger what had been happening, and that was why he sent you that text message on Friday afternoon asking you to come and see him yesterday morning. Did you realise immediately what he wanted to see you about? Is that why you went equipped with the hammer, intending to kill him?'

'No! No, none of this is true. I didn't steal any money, I didn't get any text, I didn't go to the house. I didn't do any of it!'

'Okay, Amy. We're going to speak to the Crown Prosecution Service shortly. We have to be guided by them on what happens next, but we're going to recommend you be charged with the murder of Roger Walker. Do you want to comment on that?'

I shake my head, and try to hold onto my breathing as a tear escapes my closed eyelids and rolls down my cheek.

27

Simon Robinson stared at the figures on the computer screen in front of him. There could be no denying it: they just didn't add up. He'd gone over and over them, time and time again, but there was just no way this could be made to look normal.

He didn't want to query it with Brendan or Amy. That would set alarm bells ringing. He'd decided the best course of action was to go straight to his boss.

He knocked on the door of David's office and waited for the instruction to come in.

'Morning, David,' he said, as he walked in.

'Hi Simon. How's things? What can I do for you?'

Simon gestured towards a chair.

'Sit, by all means,' David said.

Simon sat down in the chair and exhaled heavily. 'It's about the Walker account.'

David nodded. 'Alright. Go on.'

'I don't really know how to say this. I've been doing the figures on it for their year end stuff. There were bits that didn't add up, so I had to dig down a bit further.'

David leaned in towards him and cocked his head. 'Right.'

'Look, I'm sure it's all just a mistake. Probably some awkward filing or an error somewhere along the line. But there were certain categories of expenditure that had increased quite heavily over the last year or two. Things we'd expect them to have mentioned. I looked into it to get some more detail, and there are quite a few invoices to suppliers we hadn't seen before. I googled some of them but couldn't find any information. That made me a bit suspicious, so I phoned a couple of them. I don't know what I was going to say, but I just had a funny feeling. Some of them weren't real phone numbers, and the ones that were weren't for those companies.'

David sighed heavily and rubbed his chin. 'So what, you're thinking some sort of false invoicing fraud?'

'Looks like it.'

'And these invoices have been paid out?'

'Yeah. I don't know where yet. None of the invoices had account numbers or sort codes on them. That was another thing I found a bit odd. We'll need to go through everything in fine detail to track where the payments actually went.'

David stayed silent for a few moments, then spoke quietly, almost in a whisper. 'How much?'

'Difficult to say until I've been through every single invoice and payment, but from what I've found so far it's at least sixty-five thousand pounds.'

'Christ.'

'Yeah. I didn't quite know how to tell you, or what to do. It's not something I've ever seen before.'

'Well we can't let on to Amy and Brendan that we've spotted something. It's only a small company, so the odds are that at least one of them is involved with it.'

'Amy does the books,' Simon said. 'So it has to be her at a minimum. Possibly Brendan if he's in on it and has asked her to do it. But she's the only one there with access to the bookkeeping software.'

David nodded slowly. 'Jesus Christ, why would she do such a stupid thing?'

'I don't know,' Simon said. 'I was thinking maybe it'd be best to speak to Roger about it. He's still got a large stake, and he set up the company. Besides which, you're both old friends so maybe you'll be able to approach it with him in a different way.'

'Mmmm. Probably for the best. I just don't get why she would do that. The company's been doing fine, hasn't it?'

Simon nodded. 'Would've been even better with the extra sixty-five grand in their account.'

David stayed silent for a moment. 'I'll call Roger.

Christ knows what I'll say to him, though. He'll be devastated. It'll blow the family apart.'

'Maybe just call him and ask him to come into the office,' Simon said. 'We can both have a chat with him and I can explain what I've found. We'll put it in a matter-of-fact way and let him draw his own conclusions. That's probably safest. We don't want to go wading in with any accusations at this stage, even though there doesn't appear to be anyone else in the frame.'

David nodded. 'No, you're right. We've got to approach this sensibly. Are you sure you wouldn't mind being in on the meeting? It's very kind of you to offer.'

'Not at all,' Simon replied. 'Like I said, it's probably best to just lay down the facts and go from there. That's all we can do. We're not in a position to accuse anyone. We can just point out that we feel he has a right to know as the company's founder and a major shareholder.'

David forced a small smile. 'Thanks, Simon. You're a good lad. We'd be lost without you.'

Simon returned the smile, this one completely genuine. 'Honestly, don't mention it. Just doing my job. It's only fair that justice is done.'

28

'Sorry I couldn't get here any sooner,' Roger said, wiping his shoes on the mat as he was welcomed into the offices of the accountancy firm. 'I was out fishing and left my phone in the car. Your message sounded pretty urgent, though. What's the matter?'

'It's alright,' David said, greeting him at the door. 'I hope I didn't alarm you.'

'Well, a little bit. I don't think you've ever asked me to come in straight away before now.'

David shuffled awkwardly. 'Well, sometimes you just want to get things done, while they're still fresh in your mind.'

Roger stopped and looked at him. 'I've known you most of my life, David. I know when you're talking out of your arse.'

David forced an awkward smile and ushered Roger

down the corridor towards his office. 'Let's pop in here, shall we? Tea? Coffee?'

'Why, is it going to be a long one?' Roger asked.

David let go of the breath he'd been holding in. 'It might.'

'Better make it two sugars, then.'

David indicated for one of the office juniors to fetch the drinks, and the two of them and Simon seated themselves around David's desk.

'So what's this all about?' Roger asked. 'Something to do with the company, I presume? No, wait. You're not closing down, are you?'

'No, no. Nothing like that,' David said.

Simon interjected, seeming to sense that this conversation might need someone to steer it. 'I've been sorting out the year end stuff for the company,' he said. 'I noticed that quite a few of the expenses categories were a lot higher than they've been in other years. It seemed odd, because it didn't quite fit the usual pattern.'

'Well, they're trying to move the company in a new direction, modernise it. Things are bound to change,' Roger said.

Simon clenched his jaw. 'Yes, but these weren't the sort of things we would have expected. I had a closer look at the invoices the expenditure referred to, and they seemed a bit... odd.'

'Odd?'

'Yeah. They didn't have any payment reference details

on them, and the format of them looked pretty similar, even though they were apparently from six or seven different companies. And when I tried contacting those companies or looking them up online, I couldn't find any trace of them.'

Roger fell silent. All that could be heard was the sound of his breathing, which seemed to get heavier and heavier. David had only seen Roger get angry once or twice in his life, and it usually followed this calm-before-the-storm pattern.

'There's got to be some sort of innocent explanation,' Roger said.

David looked at Simon, who then spoke again. 'The companies don't exist. They've been paying out money to suppliers who aren't real.'

'How much?' Roger asked, quietly.

'We don't know for definite, but it's at least sixty-five thousand.'

Simon watched Roger's Adam's apple bobbed as he swallowed. 'And where's the money gone?'

'We don't know,' Simon replied. 'We'd have to get that information from the bank or look back through statements, although I imagine those would only show payee names. Lots of banks don't even cross-check those. You could pay a bill in the name of Mickey Mouse and it'd go through.'

Simon watched Roger's face as he digested what he'd just been told. Roger was the sort of man who tended to keep his emotions under wraps for the most part. He'd run his business successfully for many years, and was very process-driven. When it came to family and friends, though, he was the most supportive person you could ask for. He rewarded loyalty strongly, and Simon imagined it must have sent a dagger through his heart to now be realising that his family were potentially involved in a fraud which could have cost him money.

'Do we know who's responsible?' Roger asked, not looking at either of them.

'No,' David said, pausing for a moment. 'Although we believe Amy is the only person with access to the book-keeping package.'

Roger nodded slowly. 'And there's no other possibility?'

David swallowed. 'Not that we can see, Roger.'

'If I may?' Simon said, raising his hand slightly.

Roger gave an almost imperceptible nod.

'I think it might be best to have a chat with Amy off the record,' Simon said. 'Perhaps sit her down and point out what's been discovered, and see what she says. It wouldn't do any good to get heavy at this stage. As you say, there might be a totally innocent explanation. I can't for the life of me see how, but we should at least give her the benefit of the doubt.'

Roger nodded slowly. 'You're right. I'll go into the office on Monday.'

Simon shuffled awkwardly and deliberately. 'Ah, I

don't think that would be the best way to play it, if you don't mind me saying. If things do kick off, I don't think the office is the best place to do it. And anyway, she might feel cornered if you turn up there. I think some slightly more neutral ground would be better. And if I might say so, I think it might be better to strike while the iron's hot. I don't think it would do anyone any good to let bad feeling fester. I think sitting down with her and a cup of tea in the next day or so would be the best way to play it. Not today, I don't think. Maybe best to sleep on it first, but don't let it fester. If that makes any sense.'

'It does,' Roger said.

'Maybe ask her to pop over to yours tomorrow morning. That won't raise any suspicions, seeing as you're her father-in-law. It'll keep it friendly and neutral and should diffuse the situation. Hopefully you'll be able to get to the bottom of it, then.'

'Yes. You're right. Good idea. Thanks. I'll call her now.'

'Ah. I think maybe a text might be a better idea,' Simon said. 'It's just… Well, I hope you don't mind me saying, but you do sound a little… angsty. I mean, that's totally understandable in the situation, of course, but I don't think we want to give her any cause for suspicion and the time to concoct an excuse. I think the element of surprise will reveal more than anything else. I hope that didn't come across the wrong way.'

'No, not at all,' Roger said. 'Thank you.' He took his

phone out of his pocket and spent the next few minutes tapping out and deleting the message, before finally sending it.

'Done?' David asked.

Roger exhaled heavily. 'Done.'

29

Amy was starting to get sick of sitting in this musty flat, which stank of fags and booze — and worse. It was one of the reasons why she only saw Lewis once every few days at best — he barely left the flat unless it was to get more booze, and even then he'd quite happily send Greg off to get it for him.

'We should go out somewhere,' Amy said, the same as she'd said a thousand times before.

'Like where?' Lewis said. 'There's nowhere to go round here. It's shit.'

'I dunno. Go and see a film or something. Walk round the park, I dunno.'

'Yeah, walking, great.'

'Sit in the park then.'

'We're sitting here. Here's got a TV, too.'

'There's a party in town later. Some friend of Alex's,

if you want to come,' Greg said. Lewis shot him a look that Amy probably wasn't meant to see.

'Nah, I can't do tonight,' Amy said, detecting that perhaps she wasn't as welcome as Greg had made out. 'Maybe another time.'

'I think it's lads only, anyway,' Lewis said, not taking his eyes off Greg.

'I'm not sure it is,' his friend replied, holding his stare.

'Honestly, it's fine,' Amy said, trying to break this daft standoff. They could be like this sometimes, Lewis and Greg. She had no idea why. It was just boys being boys.

'He's always been a bit like this,' Lewis said, looking at Greg but talking to Amy. 'Says and does things, then thinks about them later. That's the problem with Greg. He's not a planner. Not a thinker.'

'I think maybe you should stop talking until the weed's worn off,' Greg said, quietly.

Lewis made a noise halfway between a sigh and a snort, still holding his gaze. 'He's been like this ever since we were kids. We used to spend a lot of time together. Especially in the school holidays. His mum used to take us out on trips. Denton Lakes was always a favourite. Until the last time.'

Amy gritted her teeth and tried not to say anything. She really hoped Lewis wasn't about to invoke Greg's dead mother and have a dig at her murder.

'I've never been there since that last time,' Lewis said to Greg. 'Have you?'

Greg's voice was almost a whisper. 'You know I haven't.'

'Maybe we should take a trip back there at some point. It might be good for you to see the old place again. Help you come to terms with things. Maybe exorcise some of those demons.'

Greg stood up quickly, throwing the coffee table over in the process. For a moment Amy thought he was about to attack Lewis, but he walked straight past him.

'I'm going to my room,' he said, walking down the short corridor towards his bedroom.

Lewis raised his eyebrows, took a deep breath and looked at Amy. 'See? That's the sort of person we're dealing with here.'

Amy looked back at him and said nothing. All she had were her thoughts, thoughts that Lewis had no idea how misguided yet accurate his words were.

30

I've always wondered how defence solicitors can sleep at night. The vast majority of their clients must be as guilty as sin. And they must know it, deep down. But they still have to go out and defend those people and do all they can to keep them out of prison. How do they manage to reconcile that?

But now I know there must be more people like me, people who've been wrongly arrested for something they didn't do, or who've been set up for a crime they didn't commit.

I don't know if Brian believes me. I don't think I'd believe me if I was in his shoes. Everything is so one-sided. I've got nothing. Everything has been stacked against me and I can't see a way out.

I'm almost resigned to the fact. I feel a strange sort of acceptance, knowing that I'm going to be charged with murder. Accepting that there's not a jury in the land that wouldn't be convinced by the weight of evidence against me. I'm not about to give up fighting, but I know there's no way I can win.

I wondered if perhaps this might be some elaborate setup, perhaps as part of one of those TV programmes. But that possibility disappeared the moment I spoke to Brendan. He's a dreadful actor, and there's no way what I heard in his voice was anything but genuine.

This is real. It's too real. And there's no way I can escape from it.

I'm taken from my cell and back into the side room to speak with Brian.

'I think it's time we talk through the next steps,' Brian says. 'We need to be frank and realistic about what happens from here. The police will call the CPS and they'll outline what's happened, the evidence they have against you and will request that they authorise a murder charge. Personally, I expect that'll be granted.'

'But it might not be?' I ask.

Brian cocks his head slightly and flicks his eyebrows upwards. 'It might not be. You're right. We never know how these things will go, and I've seen some pretty cut-and-dried cases go the opposite way to what one might expect, but it's rare.'

'But there's a chance?'

'There's always a chance. But if the CPS think the

evidence is strong enough to go to court, and in my opinion I think it is, then they'll authorise a charge.'

'And if they don't? I'll be free?'

'Potentially, yes. Although you can be re-arrested and charged if further evidence comes to light in the future. And the family would have the right to request a review and petition the decision under the Victims' Right to Review scheme.'

I look at him, open-mouthed. 'My family.'

'Roger's family,' Brian says.

'It's the same thing.'

'I know. And that's what makes this case so delicately balanced. The CPS will take all of that into account, but their remit is to act in the public interest — not in that of the victims, the accused or the police. They're a wholly independent body.'

'How can they be if I don't get to put my side of things to them?' I ask. 'If it's only the police who can present their evidence to the CPS, how can the CPS be independent?'

'Because they're looking at the prosecution case. You're innocent until proven guilty, particularly in the eyes of the CPS. If the police can convince them they have enough evidence to go to court, they'll do so. If they don't, you remain innocent. You don't have to prove your innocence at this stage. They have to prove your guilt.'

Before I realise what's happening, my face is on the table and I'm howling and wailing like a baby. It all comes flooding out of me, the anger, the hurt, the sheer injustice. Sadness at Roger's death, panic at the situation I'm in, exasperation at not being able to change a thing about it.

Brian does his best to comfort me, but it's not much use. There's something in his eyes, something which I think might mean he believes me, if only a bit.

'I'm so lost, Brian.'

'I know. But somebody killed Roger. And if it wasn't you, it was someone who wanted to make it look like you. Why would someone do that?'

'Because they wanted to ruin me,' I say, as if it's the most obvious answer in the world.

'It's someone who had access to the house. That leaves you and Brendan. Brendan was at the football, and CCTV shows you heading towards and leaving the scene. As does an independent witness. And as for motive...'

'It wasn't me, Brian,' I say. 'Believe me, no-one can see how bad this looks more than I can. None of it makes any sense. How can someone see me there, and how can I appear on CCTV if I wasn't there?'

Brian raises his eyebrows slightly. 'Witnesses can be unreliable. Especially elderly ones. CCTV, like any technology, can be doctored. False timestamps, maybe? But the footage was from independent town council cameras, which doesn't help us much. And both pieces of evidence combined together? Not great. Especially with everything else. Amy, if you've been set up for this, someone has planned it well. And I mean extraordinarily well. This is

THE PERFECT LIE   161

months of planning, if not years — especially if the whole invoice fraud thing was part of it.'

'It was,' I say, noting how he looks at me. 'I had nothing to do with any of it. I swear.'

'Then there's no escaping the fact that the most likely suspect is your husband.'

I shake my head. 'No, no. It wasn't Brendan. I know it wasn't.'

'People can surprise,' Brian says. 'People like this are very rarely suspected before they're actually uncovered. They manage to live two lives, almost.'

'No, I know my husband. And he was at the football, with the boys. In the other car.'

Brian smiles, but it's not a pleasant smile. It's almost condescending. 'Amy, if someone's been able to make it look like you were in places you weren't, it's entirely possible they made it look like *they* were in places *they* weren't.'

I shake my head. 'But why? He's got no reason to want to do that. Why the hell would he want to frame me? I'm his wife.'

'Maybe he was the root of the invoice fraud. He's the managing director, isn't he?'

'Well, yes, but…'

'So it's quite possible he was responsible. Maybe he felt the net closing in, knew it was going to come back to him. Saw the finger of suspicion pointing at you and decided to act out of self-preservation.'

'He wouldn't do that,' I repeat.

'You'd be amazed what people are capable of in order to defend themselves or their reputation.'

I consider this for a moment. 'But Roger only sent the text on Friday afternoon. The meeting was Saturday morning. You said this would have taken months or years of planning.'

'Yes, but it's possible he had a contingency plan ready in the back of his mind in case he was caught. It might have just been a case of putting it into action at the right time.'

I shake my head again. 'No. No, it doesn't feel right. He wouldn't do that to me. Brendan's an honourable man. He once drove off from a petrol station without paying and he was absolutely mortified. When he realised, he went back down there the next day and brought all the staff wine and flowers to apologise. There's no way he's been stealing money from the company. He didn't need to. It was doing well.'

'No gambling habits, addictions, anything like that?'

'No! Jesus Christ, just go and meet him, will you? You'll see within about thirty seconds this is all ludicrous.'

Brian sighs. 'If not him, it has to be someone else. Is there anyone else who might fit the bill? Someone who has such a dreadful vendetta against you that they'd go to this amount of effort to have you sent down for a murder you didn't commit?'

I shake my head before even thinking. 'No, of course

not. I mean…' A jolt of something surges through my chest. It almost feels like a light, a ray of hope. 'Well, there's one possibility but I don't think—'

The sound of the door opening quickly eradicates that hope, as do the words that come out of Jane McKenna's mouth.

'Hi, Amy. I just wanted to let you know that we've spoken with the Crown Prosecution Service. They've recommended that we formally charge you with the murder of Roger Walker.'

31

He pulled up a hundred yards or so down the lane from the house, knowing he was out of view of any neighbours. Not that there were many around here.

It thrilled him to be walking this route again, knowing it was time to put the next phase of his plan into action. She couldn't have set it up for him any better. The house was practically in the middle of nowhere, and the tall hedges that bordered the property and its front garden made his life one hell of a lot easier.

As he approached the property, he reached into the shrubbery and pulled out the phone, a small handful of dirt coming with it. He didn't mind. He didn't want to break his stride.

He carried on a few steps further, to the edge of the copse that bordered the front of her property. This way he was hidden from sight, yet still on the boundary.

He tapped the screen to bring it to life, then slid his finger across to unlock the phone.

One text message. Perfect.

He opened it and read it.

HI AMY. Just wondered if you could pop over tomorrow morning for an hour or so. Wanted to go through some work stuff with you.

HE TAPPED the bottom of the screen to bring up the keyboard, then typed out his reply.

YES, no problem. Will be there for 9.

HE HIT the blue arrow to send the message, and watched as the word *Delivered* appeared next to it on the screen. He allowed himself a small smile of satisfaction, knowing the message had reached its recipient. And no-one would be any the wiser.

It was too late now. There was no going back. The trail had been laid, and he had only two more things he needed to do. These were the big ones, though, and they had to wait until tomorrow. Time was of the essence. It was vital, in fact. Any deviation from the plan could bring it all crashing down.

The phone showed 65% battery. He took the portable charger out of his pocket and plugged it into the phone, before retracing his steps back past the house.

As he reached the shrubbery again, he used his jacket sleeve to wipe the device clear of prints, then placed the phone and portable charger back in its hiding place, and swiftly covered it with leaves and dirt.

He couldn't believe his luck. This was all going perfectly to plan. He knew he had to keep a calm and level head, though. He couldn't afford to get too far ahead of himself.

Up until now there'd been no real risk. Not anything which would be catastrophic if he'd been caught. But the next stage would change all of that. The next step was a big one. *The* big one.

He'd planned it all out in his head. He was confident. There could be any number of unknown variables that might come into play, but his methodology would cover most of them. It wouldn't matter too much if he was seen. Might help, even.

Anyone else might feel guilty or apprehensive, but not him. All he felt was an enormous sense of excitement. It was something he hadn't felt since Christmas Eve as a child, the pure thrill of knowing that when he woke up it would be Christmas Day. He wouldn't sleep tonight, either.

He'd been waiting far too long for this moment. He was owed it. The credit line had run out, and there was no way he was going to go another day without the enormous debt being repaid.

Tomorrow was Christmas Day. Tomorrow was the day Roger Walker died.

32

He had to be especially careful this time. If he was seen, it was entirely possible he might draw more than a quick glance.

He'd been careful, though, not to overdo it. Sure, the jeans were tight and the shoes were undeniably feminine, but he didn't want to push his luck too far.

All he had to do was hope he didn't bump into anybody. It wasn't likely, but he still had to be vigilant.

He thanked his lucky stars she lived on a quiet lane. If this had been a busy road, or if she'd had lots of neighbours, it would have been impossible.

He parked the car a little further down the lane than usual. It would be too risky to park nearby now.

Getting out of the car, he let the hair fall in front of his face, obscuring it slightly from anyone who might see him. Then he locked the car and walked calmly and confidently up the lane toward her house.

As he reached the house, he felt the sun beating down on him. Everything was falling into place just perfectly. So many times, over so many emails, he'd asked her what her plans were for that weekend. And so many times she'd told him the same thing. Saturday morning was *her* time. She'd either be in the bath or in the garden, weather permitting.

And it looked very much like the weather was permitting.

He glanced momentarily at the car on the driveway. The familiar-looking Ford Fiesta, registration FO17 UTA, in Blazer Blue. He smiled to himself. Not a bad little car, but far too noisy for him. Handled like a bag of shit, too.

With no further ado, he put his hand into the conifers and pulled out the mobile phone. The charging pack had emptied itself, but the phone was showing a full 100% battery. That'd keep it going for long enough, he was sure.

He pocketed the phone and charging pack, then made his way back down the lane towards his car.

He couldn't help but grin when he saw it. It was, he thought, the most ingenious part of his plan. His masterstroke. Two hundred and fifteen pounds a month's worth of masterstroke.

But it was perfect. A Ford Fiesta, Blazer Blue, registration FO17 UTA.

Oh yes. It was all coming together nicely now.

33

He parked the car down the lane again, then removed the wig and the brassiere. They would have already done their job, if they'd been needed.

There were two things he needed to do now, but one was far more important than the other.

He took her mobile phone out of his satchel, wrapped it in the piece of cloth and gave it a rub to make sure there were definitely no fingerprints on it.

He got out of the car and walked the rest of the way up the lane to her house. When he got there, he peered over the privet hedge, which gave a slight view of some of the garden. The weather was nice, and the parasol was up. That was a good sign. He pulled the polythene bag with the hammer inside out of his satchel. Grabbing hold of the hammer's handle through the bag, he opened it, pulled it back over the metal and launched the hammer over the bushes and into the woodland, keeping hold of the bag.

He peered in through the window of the living room, as well as through the frosted glass of the front door. He couldn't see any signs of life, so he decided to take the plunge.

He took the key from his pocket and gently, carefully, silently unlocked the door and opened it, before pushing it to behind him.

He quickly went into the downstairs toilet, and went to put the phone behind the radiator. It was too thin, would slide down and hit the floor.

He bunched the cloth up on one side of the phone, making it thicker, then tried again. Perfect. Time to leave.

He'd only just got the front door open again when he heard noises from inside the house. It sounded like another door closing. The back door. He stepped outside and pulled the door closed as silently as he could, holding it there. He stayed ducked behind the brickwork, holding the door closed, as he heard her go into the downstairs toilet.

Shit. Shit. This wouldn't do. She couldn't be finding the phone now. That would not play into his hands.

A few seconds later, he heard the sound of the toilet flushing and the toilet door closing again. He peered through the frosted glass and saw her figure walking away, back towards the back of the house and the garden.

He gave it thirty seconds or so, then took the key back out of his pocket and silently locked the door.

He walked back to his car with a sense of urgency, but without wanting to look as though he was running. He didn't want to stand out in anyone's memory or give somebody cause for concern.

When he got back to the car, knowing he was out of sight of any houses, he yanked the front and back number plates off the car. They took a bit of effort to get off, but he managed it.

He popped open the boot and put them in, taking out the two original number plates, ready with new sticky tabs on the back. He peeled off the backing on each of them, then stuck them back in their original places. The car was no longer FO17 UTA.

His involvement was complete. He'd done everything he needed to do. Now all he had to do was wait.

This was going to be the fun bit.

34

'What happens next?' I ask Brian, once the tears have stopped flowing and I've managed to regain enough control to speak.

'You'll stay here until tomorrow morning, when you'll be taken to the magistrates' court. With a murder charge, that's just a formality. Magistrates can't deal with murder charges, so it'll just be a case of giving your name and address and the case will be referred to the Crown Court. You won't even have to enter a plea at this stage, because the magistrate will automatically refer it to the Crown Court. The likelihood is you'll then be placed on remand until the Crown Court trial.'

I blink a few times, trying to take it all in. 'What does that mean?'

'Being on remand?'

I nod.

'It means the magistrate believes bail should be refused. That usually happens if it's a repeat or dangerous offender, but usually happens automatically in the case of murder.'

The words jolt through my chest like a steel bolt. 'You mean I won't be able to go home?'

'No. Sorry. I think we have to prepare ourselves for that likelihood. You'll be taken to a women's remand prison until the trial.'

The thought is pure hell. I can't go to prison. I haven't done anything wrong. 'How long will it be until the trial?'

Brian raises his eyebrows and shrugs. 'They say six to eight weeks, but there's a backlog at the moment. It could be anything up to three months until a trial begins.'

My jaw drops, and I feel my chest heaving. 'I can't do that. I can't spend three months in prison. I haven't done anything! How the hell can that be fair? I can't wait that long for them to realise this is all a massive mistake. What about my boys?'

'They'll be with their father.'

Desperation floods through me. I feel as though I'm being held underwater, unable to breathe and without the ability to do anything about it. I can't reach the surface, can't even see it. The water is pushing at my lips, ready to rush down into my lungs. I can't control it. 'Can I see them? I need to see them.'

'They'll be able to visit you while you're on remand. There are regular visiting hours.'

'Will I be able to see them alone?'

'That depends what you mean by alone,' Brian says. 'It'll be in a large room with all the other visitors and prisoners.'

I deflate, all the air pushed out of my lungs. I've got nothing left. You see these things on TV, the stark prison visiting rooms, and always assume it's been dramatised. I had no idea it was actually real.

I can't get across to Brian how unfair this all is. There's no way I can make him believe that I haven't done anything. Somehow, the evidence is overwhelming. Everything is overwhelming. I'm even starting to believe it myself. But what I can't believe is that I'm going to have to go to prison, potentially for months, before I'll even get the chance to put my side of the story forward and protest my innocence.

'I thought I was meant to be innocent until proven guilty,' I say.

'Yes, well this is where the lines get blurred, slightly. When it comes to murder it's deemed that remand is the default option. The thresholds for a charge are so high, your guilt is more or less assumed at this stage.'

'Default?' I say. 'So there is a possibility of bail?'

Brian sighs heavily. 'It'd be disingenuous of me to say yes. It is possible, in the strictest sense of the word. It has been known. But I would say it's remarkably unlikely in your case. Where would you go?'

'Back home,' I say. It doesn't even require thinking about.

'Exactly. The family home. With your husband and children. But don't forget they're not just your husband and children any more. In the eyes of the prosecution they're the son and grandchildren of a murder victim. How likely do you think it is that they're going to send the accused to live with them?'

'Somewhere else then. A hotel,' I say.

'Not going to happen, I'm afraid. It'll be deemed far too risky.'

I'm not exactly disappointed by Brian's response to that. The thought of being on the outside, but cooped up in a hotel room, even closer to my family and still unable to see them or contact them would be even worse. At least in prison I'm protected from that particular torture.

I sit for a few minutes, unable to talk or even comprehend any real thoughts. I just exist, images and sounds flashing through my mind as I try to make sense of it all.

'There really is no way out, is there?' I ask Brian.

Brian purses his lips and exhales through his nose. 'No. No, I'm afraid there isn't. Not unless we can convince the police or CPS to drop the charges. But that'll only happen if we can compile enough evidence either to prove that you can't have committed the crime, or that someone else did.'

As he says this, I think back to the conversation we

were having before McKenna came in here and told me I was being charged. I was about to tell him about Lewis.

'There is one person I think could be behind it,' I say quietly.

Brian looks at me. 'Go on.'

'It was a long time ago. And I don't think he's even… I don't know. It doesn't seem likely, but it's all I can think of.'

Brian leans forward. 'Tell me everything, Amy.'

35

'It'll be fine,' Lewis said, slapping Greg playfully on the back. 'She won't have to stay all night.'

Greg looked at the girl Lewis had his arm round. He had no idea what she'd been taking, but it wasn't just alcohol. Knowing these sorts of house parties, it could have been anything.

At parties like this, anything was fair game. He'd seen people inhaling deeply from jerry cans, drinking cleaning products and injecting god-knows-what into each other, all in the quest to get that next big hit.

Those sorts of things had never interested Greg. He drank, of course, and he'd done the odd bit of puff, but never anything stronger than that. Just enough to fit in and not look too much of a dick at parties.

This girl, though, had clearly pushed the boundaries tonight. Greg had no idea who she was — he doubted

Lewis did either. And he doubted Lewis even thought twice about Amy the whole evening. As far as Lewis was concerned, he was going to get his leg over one way or the other. It was first-come-first-served. Amy just had the right of first refusal.

Lewis leaned in towards him, his arm still round the girl's shoulders. 'I mean, come on mate. She's clearly gagging for it. And you said you wanted to head home soon anyway.'

It was no use trying to argue with Lewis. He'd always find a way of spinning it so it didn't seem so bad, or so Greg might even feel it was his idea.

Greg sighed. 'I'll grab my coat.'

He headed into the spare bedroom, where everyone had dumped their jackets and coats, and rummaged around to find his, trying to ignore the chap being fellated only inches away. Once he'd found it, he made a quick exit and joined Lewis and the mystery girl on the street outside.

Three minutes or so later, they were back at their flat, and Greg watched as Lewis attempted to fumble with the keys. He wasn't going to offer his help; Lewis could damn well ask for it.

After a few seconds, Lewis managed to get the door open, and the three of them went inside the flat.

'I'll get some music on. Greg, sort the drinks mate.'

Greg gritted his teeth, then poured three strong

measures of vodka, into which he added three splashes of coke.

The familiar sound of Lewis's favourite hard-house CD filled the flat, and Lewis threw himself down onto the sofa, the girl beside him.

Within a minute, he was clambering over her, trying to get her clothes off.

'I think you owe me another couple of drinks first,' the girl said, slurring slightly, the first words Greg had heard from her all night.

Lewis looked at Greg and raised his eyebrows momentarily, before flicking his eyes over towards the kitchen. The three downed their drinks, and Greg went to refill the glasses.

A couple of minutes later he came back with three glasses, one for each of them. Lewis stood up and went into the kitchen, before returning with the vodka bottle.

'I think we can fill these up, don't you?' he said, unscrewing the cap and filling each of the glasses right to the brim.

He pushed a glass across the coffee table to the girl, and one to Greg, then carefully lifted his into the air as if proposing a toast, a small splash of vodka and coke running down his hand.

'Wait, wait. What are we toasting?' the girl said.

Lewis looked at her. 'How about... good times?'

The girl smiled. 'To good times.'

The three of them downed their drinks in one. Even Greg was starting to loosen up now.

The girl leaned over and started to kiss Lewis. He played along for a moment or two, then pulled away.

'Wait. I thought you said you needed a couple more drinks. That was only one more.'

The girl shrugged. 'What can I say? I'm a cheap date.'

Greg watched as they started kissing again. Within seconds, they had their hands down each other's trousers, and Greg was starting to get aroused. He watched as both pairs of trousers came down and Lewis climbed on top of the girl, kissing her constantly.

'No, stop,' she said, as Lewis pulled her knickers aside and started to have sex with her. 'I said stop.'

'It's alright. Don't worry. Just enjoy it,' Lewis replied, grunting. 'Greg, come and get a load of this. You don't mind if my mate joins in do you?' he said to her, as if he'd almost forgotten she was there.

The girl didn't reply. Greg stood up and walked over to them. He was tempted. Very tempted. But he could see she wasn't exactly enjoying herself.

Without warning, the girl became hysterical and started screaming.

Greg reacted instinctively. He put his hand over the girl's mouth. 'Stop it! Be quiet. They'll fucking hear you next door.'

The girl started flailing her arms around, but Greg

managed to dodge them. Lewis, meanwhile, kept thrusting away, seemingly enjoying the commotion. He spoke only between animalistic grunts.

'Don't fucking let her go, Greg. Keep her there. That's it.'

Greg could feel the warmth and moisture of the girl's breath on his hand as he kept it clamped firmly over her face. She started to buckle and kick.

'Fucking hold her down!' Lewis barked.

Greg did as he was told. He leaned across and put his arm across her neck, pinning her to the sofa. He closed his eyes and tried to blot out the noise and the sight of the girl writhing in desperation. In a moment of desperation, he started reciting songs from Bugsy Malone in his head, trying to blank out what was going on.

He didn't know how long he did it for, but he was brought back into the here and now by Lewis tapping him on the shoulder. 'Mate. I'm done,' he said, pulling up his pants and fetching his trousers from the floor.

Greg stood up and wiped his hands on his trousers.

He looked back down at the girl, lying on the sofa, her legs open. Just moments earlier she'd been a screaming, quivering wreck. But now she was still.

Too still.

She was dead.

36

He felt the reassuring crunch of the tyres on the gravel as he reversed onto Roger's driveway. This way, it'd be a lot easier to get out again in a few minutes' time.

He pulled close to the house, making sure the registration number of the car wouldn't be seen from inside.

He leaned across and picked up the satchel from the passenger-side footwell of the car, making sure it was securely fastened. He'd had to remove the items and put them in the bag whilst coasting slowly up Roger's road, which hadn't been easy.

He got out and stepped onto the gravel, then made his way quickly across the footpath to the front door.

Five steps.

He rang the doorbell and waited for the answer. Fifteen seconds later, it came.

'Simon,' Roger said, opening the door. 'Hi, come in.'

Simon did as he was told.

'I didn't know you were going to be here,' Roger said. 'I thought it was just me and Amy.'

Roger always was the perfect diplomat. *I didn't know you were going to be here.* Never *What the hell are you doing here?* That was the sort of thing that made him a people person, and was one of the reasons why he'd been so well-liked.

He liked him too, if he had to be honest. That's why he felt a small pang of regret at what he now had to do. Only a small one, mind. That feeling was almost completely overwhelmed by the absolute necessity and justice that would be done by committing this act.

'It is, but I was having a bit of a closer look at things last night, and I think there are one or two things you might want to know before she turns up.'

Roger nodded. 'Right, okay. Come on through to the kitchen. Would you like a drink?'

'I'm fine, thanks,' he replied. 'I won't keep you long. Promise. I just thought you might appreciate the extra information before the meeting. A bit more collateral, if you will.'

'Yes, fine. Thank you. I appreciate all your hard work on this, Simon.'

'It's fine, honestly,' he replied, looking at the man who was now sitting down at the kitchen table. The last thing he'd do. 'I just wanted to say how sorry I was that you had to find out like this. That you had to find out at all, really. That it even happened.'

'Thank you, Simon. But please, don't worry. You're doing the right thing. It wasn't your fault.'

Simon nodded slowly. 'No. No, it wasn't.'

'So you had something you wanted to give me?'

Simon snapped back to reality. 'Yes. It's in my bag,' he said, feeling the huge rush of adrenalin as he realised how quickly his moment had come.

In one swift movement, he lifted the hammer out of the bag, swung it back behind him and brought it crashing down on Roger's skull.

37

'Fuck's sake, Greg, do something mate!' Lewis yelled, his eyes red, panic written loud across his face.

'Like what?'

'I dunno, CPR or something? Chuck a glass of water over her. Anything.'

'Well I dunno how to do CPR,' Greg said. 'Do you?'

'Course I don't! Do I look a doctor to you?'

Greg looked at the girl, then looked up at Lewis. 'Mate. She's gone.'

Lewis looked down at her, then slowly started shaking his head. 'No. No. She can't be. This can't be happening.' He leaned over her and shook her by the shoulders. 'Come on, babe! Wake up!'

Greg watched as Lewis tried desperately to revive the girl, but it was no good. She was long gone.'

'Fuck! Fuck!' Lewis started pacing around the flat. 'We've got to get rid of her mate,' he said, finally.

'Wait, what? Are you serious? We can't just "get rid" of a dead body. What do you want me to do, chuck her in the bin?'

Lewis stood and thought for a moment. 'The woods,' he said. 'We'll have to bury her in the woods.'

'Mate, have you got any idea how hard that would be? And what if someone finds her? They're bound to find her.'

'Yeah, like no-one's going to spot her lying dead on our fucking sofa! Have you got any better options?'

Greg looked at Lewis. There were other options, of course, but they were all far from ideal. And they weren't ones he thought it wise to share with Lewis.

'We're gonna need to cover ourselves,' Greg said. 'Just in case she is found, and someone says they saw her with us. Did she just come in and sit straight down on the sofa? Did she go anywhere else?'

'You know she didn't! You were here!'

'I know, I know,' Greg said, putting a hand on his friend's shoulder. 'I just need to make sure we've got all angles covered, alright? Listen, you do what you need to do in the woods. I'll stay here and make sure everything's spotless. No fingerprints of hers, nothing.'

'You're not gonna help me?'

'What do you think this is?' he said, gesturing at the scene in front of them. 'This is destroying the evidence.

Making sure there's absolutely no trace or proof of her ever having been here. That way, even if someone does find her, we're covered.'

By now, Lewis was swaying unsteadily on his feet.

'Listen,' Greg said, 'I'll grab some bin bags. You go and reverse the car up to the front door. Then we'll wrap her up and put her in the boot, alright?'

Lewis nodded, and did as he was told.

'Thank fuck it's a ground-floor flat,' he slurred, as he left the room.

Once Lewis had gone out, everything was deathly silent. Greg looked down at the lifeless body of the girl, and in that moment he knew exactly what he had to do.

38

There was no doubting it — the man was dead. The attack was just enough to make absolutely certain, but without him overstaying his welcome and running the risk of being caught.

Roger had been louder than he'd expected. He'd clung on for longer, the guttural roar unexpected, but thankfully planned for.

He pulled a polythene bag out of his satchel and put the hammer inside it, before putting them both back inside the satchel. From inside, he took out a long blonde wig, a brassiere and a pair of silicone pouches. He didn't know what size the bitch's tits were, but these were small enough to be about right. The wig and sunglasses had done the job on the drive over here, but he'd have to be even more convincing now. Just in case.

He quickly assembled his costume, topping it off with a pair of dark sunglasses, and headed for the front door.

He paused for a moment. Had he touched anything? No, he'd been very careful not to. He'd shaken hands with Roger at the door, but he was pretty sure you couldn't leave fingerprints on someone else's hands. In any case, they'd been in each other's company yesterday, so minute traces of his DNA would be reasonable.

He had no time to waste. He carried on to the front door and used the satchel to push down on the handle, taking extra care not to touch anything. He slid his wrist up behind the front handle and pulled the door as hard as he could, making sure it shut fully behind him.

Five steps.

He unlocked the car, threw the satchel across onto the passenger's seat of FO17 UTA, started up the engine and floored the accelerator.

39

EIGHTEEN YEARS EARLIER.

Greg had been cagey with her on the phone, and tried to keep the call only a few seconds. He didn't know how these things worked, but he didn't want to risk the police getting hold of his mobile phone and seeing a load of panicked texts having been sent to Amy.

Fortunately for him, Amy had no qualms about sneaking out of the house at that time of night to meet him.

'What's going on?' she said, as she met him at the end of the footpath that ran along the back gardens of the road she lived on.

'Something's happened,' Greg said, gesturing for her to follow him further along the path towards the next housing estate. The last thing he wanted was for Lewis to rock up and find them. Although, he was fairly sure Lewis would be occupied for the next hour or two at least.

'What do you mean "happened"? Do you mean Lewis? Is he okay?'

Greg could sense the rising panic in Amy's voice, and he tried to placate her.

'He's fine. Yeah. He's… he's fine.'

'Then what is it?'

Greg moistened his lips and tried to think of a way to phrase it. He'd been practicing on the way over, but none of it made any sense.

'Something happened. Lewis… Lewis took a girl back to the flat earlier. After the party.'

Amy looked at him for a moment, and Greg could see the hurt in her eyes. She knew Lewis was no saint, but this was probably the first time anyone had told her outright that her boyfriend had been cheating on her.

'Did they…'

'Amy, seriously. That really isn't the most important bit right now. But yes, they did. She… She didn't want to.'

'What, he forced himself on her? He *raped* her?' Amy's voice got louder and louder.

'Sshh! Keep your voice down. Seriously. Look, I don't know how it happened, but I was in my room, and I came out and he was just standing there. And she was…'

The look in Amy's eyes told Greg she knew what came next, but she had to ask the question anyway.'

'What?'

Greg looked at the floor, then back up at Amy. 'She was dead.'

Amy's hands shot up to her mouth and her eyes slowly turned a deep shade of crimson. She took a few steps backwards, away from Greg, shaking her head, then turned and retched into the undergrowth.

'Amy, please. I'm scared. She was just… I don't know. I don't know what happened, I don't know why he did it.'

'He… he killed her?' Amy asked, her voice quiet.

Greg thought about this only for a split second. He knew there was no going back from this. He knew this was a moment that would change the course of both of their lives forever.

He nodded.

'Oh god. Oh Jesus. Where is he? What happened?'

Greg took hold of Amy's shoulders and pressed his head against hers.

'I don't know. I just ran. I didn't know what to do, Ames. I just ran. I don't know where he's gone or what he's doing.'

Amy swallowed. 'We need to ring the police.'

'And say what? "I saw my mate murdering someone so I legged it"?'

'You can say you panicked. You were scared he'd do the same to you. It's normal, Greg. Who would know what to do in a situation like that? No-one.'

Greg shook his head and took a step back.

'No. Trust me Ames, I know what he's like. I was there, in the flat. He'll make out I was some part of it.

He'll say I was involved. He'll take me down with him. I can't risk that.'

Amy looked at him. 'He wouldn't do that. Would he?'

'I've known him since we were kids. Trust me. He'd take his own grandmother down if it helped him. I can't let him do that. I wasn't in the room, Amy. I wasn't there. You have to believe me.'

'I do, I do believe you,' she said, wrapping her arms around him. 'I trust you, Greg. You're not like him.'

Greg held her for a minute or so, but it felt like an eternity. He could've stayed there forever.

'Ames, there's one thing we could do. The only way we can make sure we do the right thing and he doesn't try taking me down with him.'

'What?'

'We have to say we were together. Tonight.'

Amy's eyes narrowed. 'You want me to give you an alibi? You want me to lie to the police?'

'Amy, think about it. If we don't say that and protect ourselves, he'll only do the same but much worse. He'll make out I was there. I was in the flat, but he'll say other stuff. I know him. I'll… I'll go to prison, Ames.'

'But they can prove you didn't do anything. There's DNA and stuff, surely?'

Greg forced out a small laugh. 'Yeah. DNA. It's my flat, Ames. My DNA's all over the bloody place. That's only going to help him. The only thing we can do to protect ourselves and make sure he doesn't get away with this is to say we were together.'

Amy blinked a few times, the magnitude of what had happened and what she was being asked to do clearly visible on her face.

'But what if we get caught lying? What if they find out we weren't together?'

'How are they going to do that?' Greg asked. 'Did you see anyone else tonight?'

'Well, no.'

'Even your mum?'

'She's out. She's staying at her sister's place until tomorrow. I didn't want to tell Lewis, because… Well, you know. He'd try to use it as an opportunity, or throw a bloody party or something.'

Greg nodded. 'He would. He's a nasty piece of work. I'm sorry to have to say that, Ames.'

Amy shook her head. 'It's alright. But this… Jesus, Greg. I don't know. This is massive. This is absolutely fucking massive.'

'I know. And that's why we need to make sure we've got our story straight. We'll say I went to yours after the party. No-one knows any different, except Lewis. And… and the girl. But she's not exactly going to be giving a statement, is she? And Lewis… Well, if he's sitting there with blood on his hands he's not going to be the most credible witness. I'll say I came from the party over to yours, because Lewis had taken the girl home and I didn't want to be a spare wheel.'

Amy looked up at him. 'You know he'll never forgive us, don't you?'

Greg swallowed, then nodded. 'I know. But it's our only choice. Are you in?'

Amy took a deep breath, then let it out.

'I'm in.'

40

'How long was he sentenced for?' Brian asks.

'Eighteen years.'

'And this was, when?'

'2001. September. During the World Trade Center attacks.'

Brian nods slowly. 'Likelihood is he'll have been out a while already. Years. If this was a revenge situation, one would expect him to have acted sooner. Did the police not tell you he'd been released? Usually they inform witnesses as part of their duty of care.'

'No. I didn't need to testify in court, and to be honest I didn't want to hear any more about it. I've put it completely behind me, wiped it out of my mind almost. It's not a time in my life I wanted to go back to.'

'I understand,' Brian says. 'And what about your husband? Did you ever tell him about it?'

'No,' I say. 'Well, not in that amount of detail. I've never told anyone that amount of detail. I told Brendan I once had a boyfriend who got sent to prison for killing someone, but that was about it. I made out we hadn't been together long and that it wasn't anyone I knew, and he just kind of left it like that. I think he sensed it wasn't something I wanted to talk about.'

'And you've heard nothing from Lewis since? Or Greg?'

I shake my head. 'No. Greg moved away, but I know he's been in touch with some old friends on Facebook. They've mentioned his name, but I've not spoken to him or seen him for years.'

'What happened after the trial?' Brian asks. I can tell from his voice and body language that he's noticed there's a little more to this story.

I lean back in my chair and exhale. 'We got together. Me and Greg. Only for a few weeks. A couple of months, maybe. Then it became pretty clear it wasn't going to work. There was too much… history. Too much baggage. We couldn't be a couple with all of that looming over us.'

'Did Lewis know about this?'

I think for a moment, then nod. 'I think so. Somebody mentioned something at the time. I think a friend had gone to visit him in prison and said something to him. But like I say, I tried to keep away from it all. I never wanted to see him again. I had no intention of being back in that place. I just wanted to move on and live a normal life again.'

'And what are your thoughts about Greg?'

I was half hoping he wouldn't ask me this. There are uncomfortable thoughts I've had for a while, which I've not wanted to address. I haven't seen the point. It's all in the past, and there wouldn't have been any use in dredging up old feelings. 'I… I always wondered. Whether what he told me was true. You know?'

'Go on.'

'Well, some of it just didn't seem right. He seemed panicked. Desperate. He changed after that night. Got more cocky and arrogant. I always wondered if… Well, I wondered if what Greg told me was actually true.'

'You think he might have killed the girl? And tried to make it look like it was Lewis?'

I shrug. 'I don't know. Maybe. I think they were both there. Greg seemed to know too much. Maybe he was more involved than he claimed he was, and that's what got Lewis so angry. If to him it looked like me and Greg had colluded to cover it up and send him down for killing that girl…'

Brian mulls over what I've told him, then looks up at me. 'Okay. Well, it's a start. It's someone with a motive to want to set you up. If he feels he was set up and it was your alibi for Greg that contributed towards his conviction, that could be seen as motive enough. But we'll need more than that to overturn a murder charge. It's nowhere near as compelling as the evidence the police and CPS have against you right now.'

'And how do we do that?' I ask.

'With difficulty, if I'm honest. I think we need to speak to the police and mention this. If they think it's compelling enough, they should want to question Lewis. They'll have a record of where he's living now. Greg should be easier to track down. I'll put some wheels in motion on that front, and see if we can get hold of him. But I can't make any promises, of course.'

'I know,' I say. 'Thank you.' I can detect a slight frisson of excitement in Brian's voice. I've sensed a few times that he might just believe me, or that perhaps he could see something in my eyes. But the evidence had been so overwhelming, he had to let his head rule his heart. Now, I think perhaps I have some hope, even if it's only a tiny glimmer.

There's a knock at the door and it opens. It's McKenna.

'Magistrates' court hearing is set for nine-thirty tomorrow morning,' she says, before walking back out and closing the door.

41

Spring and autumn were always difficult seasons at this time of the morning. It'd usually be absolutely freezing cold, but quickly warm up into quite a nice day.

That didn't help Victor Crawford, though. He'd start off the day walking his dogs through the woods, battling against the cold morning chill as it tried to seep its way through his padded coat. Then he'd go back home, drop off the dogs and head back out into the bitter air on his walk to work.

Working outdoors wasn't a problem for him, but by mid-morning he found himself dripping with sweat, jettisoning layers of clothing. By home time, he'd be freezing again and it'd be back on with the padded coat.

Still, he'd be retired in five months, so he was happy enough taking the rough with the smooth for now.

His two Labradors, Bonnie and Clyde, bounded off

into the woods, running and snuffling in the brown bark and leaves, as they did every morning.

This morning, though, was ever so slightly different.

Clyde seemed to make a beeline for one particular part of the woods, deep into the copse, where none of them had ever walked. The dogs tended to stick close to the path, and rarely bolted.

'Clyde!' Victor called, in his special sharp voice, reserved for errant dogs. Every other time he'd used this, the dog had immediately turned and come back to him, trained as it had been by Victor's own fair hand.

The dog ignored him, and instead was hastily followed by Bonnie, who by now had realised that Clyde was likely onto something interesting.

Victor ducked and swerved his way past sharp branches and through overgrown brambles, until he got within a few feet of the dogs, which had now buried their way down through a good amount of soil.

They certainly had found something, but it wasn't the usual discarded toy or a perfectly-shaped stick for throwing.

This was something else.

This was something quite different.

This was a dead body.

42

The news spread quickly. By now, everyone was talking about the dead body that had been found in the woods.

There were rumours it was a girl from the next town. No names had been mentioned, but Amy had eagerly awaited the evening news — for the first time in her life — to find out what they had discovered.

She'd spent the day worrying and fretting about it. Greg had been great, though. He told her not to worry, assured her everything would be alright. Once the body was found and the identity announced, Greg would go to the police and tell them he recognised the girl. He'd say it was the girl Lewis met at the party that night, and left with. He'd tell them he didn't want to be a spare wheel, so he left them to it and went to see Amy. Amy had agreed to back him up if it came to it.

There seemed to be no way they could lose.

Amy had worried about what might happen to Lewis. But each time that worry was overtaken by absolute anger and disbelief. Anger that Lewis had gone off and slept with another girl. Disbelief that he'd actually *murdered* someone. There was no going back from that sort of thing.

She tried to keep things natural, but it was difficult. How do you behave normally when you find out your boyfriend's cheated on you and then killed the girl? She'd managed to avoid seeing him since, but it was only going to get more difficult.

She sat in her living room, with the TV news on. They were leading with a couple of other stories, but had mentioned the body in the woods at the start of the show, indicating they'd cover it later. Her heart had skipped a beat when she heard the words and saw the pictures, even though it was barely five seconds long and only showed a few police officers standing on the edge of the woods.

Suddenly it was real.

'Blimey, watching the news? Not your usual sort of thing,' her mum said, entering the room. She almost frightened the life out of Amy.

'Oh. No, it just came on after something I was watching,' Amy said, playing a game of Snake on her phone. She never really played Snake; it was just something she'd thought of to make it look less like she was bothered about the news.

'Mind if I switch it over then?' her mum said.

'No, don't,' Amy replied, perhaps a little too keenly.

'Why? You never watch the news.'

'I've never tried. It's alright. Some of it's interesting. They're trying to close one of the hospitals, apparently.'

Amy's mum gave her a look that said *Who are you and what have you done with Amy?*

'Alright. If you say so. Got to be better than most of that American rubbish you watch. At least there's no canned laughter on the news.' Her mum had a thing about canned laughter. God knows why. 'And if you really want to watch it, you can put that blooming thing down, too.'

Amy did as she was told and put her mobile phone down.

The next couple of news stories were as boring as anything. She really couldn't understand why people got so worked up about stuff. Most of this wasn't even really news. Why weren't they leading with the story about the dead body in the woods? Surely that was far bigger news than some old fart having a pop at the council for putting a lamppost in the wrong place.

And then, just as she was starting to think that perhaps they'd decided not to run with it after all, the focus switched back to the studio and they were talking about it. Amy thought that maybe they'd left it until a little later in the bulletin as it was such a fresh story, and they might have been waiting for more news to come through.

The cameras cut to a reporter at the scene. Amy watched, her eyes unblinking, as he explained the story to the viewers.

'At the moment, things are still a little unclear, with more information still to come,' the reporter said. 'But what we do know is that the body was discovered by a dog walker early this morning, and that it's believed to be that of a teenage girl. The police haven't given any clues as to her identity at the moment, but local sources are speculating links between this find and the recent disappearance of sixteen-year-old Hannah Shaw.'

The name felt like a sucker punch to the stomach for Amy. The girl had a name. Of course she did. Amy knew that. But finally hearing it made her stop being 'the girl'. She was now a person. Somebody who'd slept with her boyfriend. The boyfriend who'd then murdered her.

'It's important to say at this stage that there's been no formal identification of the body, but we understand that Hannah's parents have been informed. Judging by the police presence and the way things are being handled here, it's my assumption that a murder case will now be underway. That, then, begs the real question. Whether or not the body found in the woods today *is* Hannah Shaw, how did the girl get to be here? Was she killed here, or was her body placed here by her killer? And who would carry out such an act on a defenceless young woman in the first place? All questions which have to be asked and which, I'm sure, will be asked.'

The camera cut back to the news room.

'That's terrible, that,' Amy's mum said.

Amy tried to keep the look on her face neutral.

'Yeah, I know.'

'Hopefully no-one you know. And you wonder why I don't like you being out late at night?'

'I know, Mum. I know.'

'Never know who these people are. You never know when you're going to bump into a murderer.'

Amy swallowed hard.

She was pretty sure she did.

43

Lewis poked his tongue into the inside of his cheek, trying to hold back the anger and frustration.

He couldn't understand why they'd come straight to him. The body had only been found a few hours earlier, and he hadn't exactly left his business card with it. Even if there'd been some sort of DNA found, he'd never been arrested or had his DNA taken so he didn't see any way they would have matched it to him.

He'd hoped the body would remain undiscovered for a lot longer. He'd covered it over with leaves, bark and a few inches of mud, but hadn't fully buried it six feet down. He'd heard somewhere that was best — that the body would rot down quicker that way. He didn't know how true it was. It certainly hadn't proved to be particularly helpful in this instance.

The two police officers sat across the other side of the

table from him, the duty solicitor sitting to his left. The bloke had barely said a word since he'd turned up.

'Lewis, what can you tell me about Hannah Shaw?' the older police officer asked.

Lewis shrugged and shook his head. 'Nothing.'

'Do you know her at all? Have you heard her name before?'

Lewis looked at them for a moment, before speaking. 'No.'

'We had a call from a member of the public who said they saw you speaking to her at a party, only a few hours before she went missing. Does that ring any bells?'

Lewis shuffled slightly in his seat. 'I dunno. I spoke to a lot of people at that party. There were loads of people there. I don't remember who everyone was.'

The police officer smiled and looked away for a moment. 'Okay, well perhaps I can jog your memory slightly. We have an eyewitness who said you left the party with Hannah Shaw. Does that narrow it down a bit?'

Lewis looked at him. He didn't want to give away anything on his face, but he needed to know who'd said this to them. He tried desperately to think back to who else was at the party, who might have seen them leave, whose fucking stupid eagle eye had landed him in the nick.

He'd left the party with that girl, but he didn't know her name. Not until it had come up on the news. Greg had left with them, come back with them, so he must have been nicked too. The same witness would've given both names, surely. Most people knew the two of them.

He decided against mentioning that, though. There was still a chance the witness didn't know or couldn't name Greg, or that they hadn't seen him. He wasn't about to drag him into it if he hadn't already been nicked.

'Lewis? Do you remember leaving the party with Hannah Shaw?'

Lewis sniffed. 'I remember leaving the party with someone. I didn't know her name, though.'

'And where did you go from there?' the officer asked him.

'I don't really remember.'

'Did you go back to your flat?'

Lewis thought carefully about this. There was no doubt they would have been searching his flat. They'd probably taken swabs and samples and stuff. All they needed to do was find one hair or something and that'd be it. Could he trust Greg's clean-up job? Or was it best to come clean now and at least tell them she'd been there?

He remembered someone telling him once that the best lies were the ones which were ninety-nine percent truth. All you had to change was one small aspect of the story. Huge, elaborate cover stories tended to fall apart.

'Yeah, I think so,' he said.

'You think so?'

'I'd had a lot to drink. I don't remember much.'

The police officer nodded and wrote something down on his pad of paper. Lewis couldn't make out what it was.

'Okay. Do you remember anything that happened? Did you have a few more drinks, maybe?'

Lewis swallowed. 'Yeah, probably.'

'And then what?'

He shrugged. 'I dunno.'

Although it was best to tell them ninety-nine percent of the truth, he wasn't about to offer them anything they hadn't already come up with themselves. He had no way of knowing how much they knew, and he wasn't going to do their job for them.

'Did you have sex with her, Lewis?'

The question was direct and loaded with meaning. He seemed to be saying *I know you had sex with her, didn't you?*

'Yeah, I think so,' Lewis replied.

'You think so?'

'Like I said, I'd had a lot to drink.'

'Did you have enough to drink to remember if she consented?'

Lewis blinked a few times. 'Yeah. Of course she did.'

'So you'd had too much to drink to remember who you left the party with, to remember getting home and to remember having sex with her, but you quite clearly remembering her consenting to it?'

'Well I wouldn't have done it otherwise, would I?' Lewis said.

The police officer looked at him for a few moments.

'Well, I don't know. But I'll level with you and tell you what we do know. Hannah Shaw's body was found in woodland not too far from your flat. She was clothed on top, but naked from the waist down. We haven't found those clothes yet. There are signs of recent sexual intercourse. It seems whoever she had sex with didn't use a condom. Does that seem to fit the bill, Lewis?'

Lewis thought about this for a moment. There was nothing in that which said he'd killed her. Only that he'd had sex with her, and she'd later been found dead.

He needed to play this right.

'Well yeah, but I don't know anything about her being found dead, for Christ's sake. We finished, she left and that was the last I saw of her.'

'What time was that?' the officer asked.

He tried desperately to think back to what time this all happened. The timings needed to be real for it to make sense.

'About quarter past eleven, half eleven maybe.'

'Okay. That's interesting. Because a neighbour of yours heard some odd noises, then saw you get into your car and drive off at twenty-five past eleven. Does that sound about right?'

'Yeah, I had to go out.'

'You'd been drinking heavily, hadn't you?'

What were they going to do? Breathalyse him now? Without any direct evidence they weren't exactly about to do him for drink driving. And even if they did, it was better than murder.

Lewis ignored the question.

'Lewis, your neighbour says the front door to your flat has a very distinctive squeal when it opens. They can hear it quite clearly. They say they heard you coming home at ten-thirty. Then the next noise they heard was at twenty-five past eleven, when they looked out the window and saw you driving off in your car.'

'Uh, yeah. I remember now,' Lewis said, desperately trying to formulate a new truth. 'I left her in the flat for a bit. She said she wanted to sort herself out, have a shower and that. Get a bit to eat.'

'And you just went out and left her there, alone in your flat? A girl you'd only met a couple of hours previously? Do you know what time she left?'

Lewis shook his head. 'I dunno.'

'Your neighbour heard the front door to your flat squealing again about two or three minutes later. Might that have been her?'

'Yeah, maybe.'

'Two or three minutes is quite quick for a shower and a midnight feast, isn't it?'

'I dunno. Maybe she decided not to. Her decision.'

'Where did you go in your car, Lewis?'

Lewis thought about this for a moment. His story was starting to become seriously unstuck. He needed something, something solid, something concrete. He needed an alibi. He knew the perfect one, too. Amy would sort him out. She'd always stood by him.

She was a good girl, Amy. She knew to do the right thing. He knew if the police asked her if he'd been with her that night, she'd say yes. She'd know she would be able to run it off the rails there and then, and get him out of the shit. She'd assume it was something to do with drugs, not something like this. He'd sort all that out later.

'I went to my girlfriend's house.'

'Okay. And her name is?'

Lewis swallowed. 'Amy Hennessy.'

The police officer wrote down on his notepad again.

'So how did Hannah Shaw end up dead, Lewis? We know she was at your flat. We know you had sex with her. Then somehow she manages to leave your flat, presumably half naked unless someone else managed to pinch the bottom half of her clothing on the way, and ends up lying dead in the woods. I can't make much sense of that, can you?'

Lewis shook his head. 'I dunno.'

'You see, there are one or two problems at the moment. The forensics officers at the scene don't think Hannah was actually killed in the woods. They reckon her body was taken there after she died. There are signs that she struggled with someone, too. It looks as though she was suffocated and her windpipe was crushed, possibly by someone lying on top of her. Do you want to comment on that at all?'

Lewis thought for a moment. 'No, I don't know anything about that.'

'So you'd gone to see your girlfriend, Amy. Then Hannah walked half-naked from your flat, someone else grabbed her, pinned her to the floor, crushed her windpipe and suffocated her, then took her off to the woods and buried her?'

'I don't know,' Lewis said. 'I don't know what happened after I left, do I?'

The police officer leaned back in his seat and folded his arms.

'You see, we don't think she left your flat alive at all. We think she died in there. We think you had sex with her, then she died. What we don't know is the timelines, or what specifically happened.'

Lewis could feel his world closing in on him. He couldn't see any way he could possibly get out of this now.

'Do you live alone, Lewis?' the police officer asked him.

He suddenly felt as if he'd been thrown a lifeline.

'No, I live with my mate, Greg.'

The police officer nodded. 'And where was he? After this party, I mean. And while you went to see your girlfriend. Just to double-check. Her name's Amy Hennessy, isn't it?'

Lewis nodded. 'Yeah. Uh, he was at the party with me. Then we went back to the flat, and he went to bed.'

'So you're saying he was in the flat when you left to go and see Amy?'

'Yeah, I presume so.'

'You presume so?'

'Well I didn't go in and check on him or give him a kiss goodnight if that's what you mean.'

'But you would have heard the squeaky front door go if he'd gone out, right?'

'Probably, yeah.'

'Do you want to say anything about all this, Lewis? Because it's not looking great for you right now.'

Lewis thought long and hard for a few moments. The police officer was right. The way things were going, he was going to go down. Once they'd done the DNA match, checked CCTV. If they took swabs from the boot of his car, there was every chance there'd be a trace of Hannah's DNA in there. They might have already tested that. This all might just be a big charade to get him to admit to it.

He couldn't risk that. He had to find something, had to use something. As far as he could see, there was only one way out. It wasn't what he wanted to do. But he had to put himself first.

'Uh, well there's only one explanation then, isn't there?' he said to the police officer. 'Greg must have killed her.'

44

Amy and Greg had spoken at length about what they'd say when this happened. Greg had been right: Lewis had tried to make out it had been his fault.

Up until then, Amy had been slightly skeptical. She knew Lewis wasn't exactly Mother Teresa, but she doubted he'd try and shift the blame onto his best friend. And there'd still been that slight niggling thought that he might not have actually killed the girl.

But that had all been blown out of the window. It had played out exactly like Greg had predicted and, to Amy, that was unforgivable.

Greg had been there for her. She'd always felt like she could go to him, talk to him. She now saw that was the role Lewis should have filled, but didn't. As far as she was concerned, he deserved everything he got. Greg had been good to her, and she would repay his kindness.

Anyway, what was one little white lie to make sure justice was done?

The police had taken Greg in for questioning. He hadn't been arrested, they said — they were just interviewing him under caution. Amy didn't know what that meant. It still sounded scary, but it had to be a good thing that they hadn't arrested him.

And then the call had come.

She was pleased they'd phoned her and asked her to come in, and not just turned up on her doorstep. She had no idea what her mum would have thought if she'd answered the door to the police. Even if she wasn't in at the time, some nosy neighbour would have seen the police car and made a point of asking her later.

They'd got her number from Greg, they said, and could she pop into the police station to answer a few questions? Nothing to worry about, they said.

That didn't stop Amy worrying, though. She couldn't remember ever having been in a police station before in her life, so she had no idea what to expect. She'd seen a couple of things on TV, but that was about it.

They'd asked her for her date of birth, and she'd wound it back three years, made out she was eighteen, nearly nineteen. That way, Greg had told her, she wouldn't need an appropriate adult to attend the interview with her. The last thing she wanted was to have to tell her mum about all this. Nor did she want the usual raised eyebrows from people who found out she was only fifteen years old and going out with a guy a few years her senior.

Her local police station was a large red-brick building, imposingly situated in the centre of town. She'd always wondered how the police cars managed to get out of there to emergencies, as the traffic was always stuffed.

The inside of the building was no less imposing. The floor was hard and cold, the walls were dirty and cold and the atmosphere was just cold. One wall was almost entirely made of what Amy assumed was bulletproof glass, with two officers sitting behind it, acting as makeshift receptionists. Four or five people sat on the plastic chairs in the waiting area, spreading themselves across the room, none of them wanting to sit anywhere near another human being. Amy immediately had her nerves set on edge.

She spoke to one of the men behind the glass screen and told them who she was and what she was there for. The man asked her to take a seat. She opted to perch on the end chair, the only one which was at least two chairs away from another person, and huddled into herself.

It was only a couple of minutes before the police officer came out and introduced herself, and showed her through into the back of the police station.

They sat down in a surprisingly comfortable room. Amy didn't think this was where they interviewed the criminals, that was for sure. There were three comfortable armchairs, a low coffee table with magazines on it and a small kitchenette off to the side by the door.

'Now, as you know, there's nothing to worry about,' the police officer said. 'It's to do with a case we're currently investigating, and we're trying to piece together what happened. Your name has come up as someone who might be able to help us do that. Is that alright?'

Amy nodded. She didn't know why the woman couldn't just get straight to the point so she could answer her question and get out of here.

'Okay, do you remember where you were on the night of the fourteenth?' the officer asked.

'Uh, that was Friday, wasn't it?'

'That's right, yes.'

'At home.'

The officer wrote on her notepad. 'And was anyone else there with you?'

'No, my mum was away for the night. She doesn't like me having people round when she's not there.'

The police officer smiled. 'Very sensible too. Did you see anyone else at all that night?'

'Oh, yeah, I did,' Amy said, as if it had just passed her as an afterthought. 'A friend of mine came over about half ten, something like that.'

The officer smiled again. 'Don't worry, I won't tell your mum. What's your friend's name?'

Amy swallowed. 'Greg. Greg Lawrence.'

'And where had Greg been?'

'At a party. He said he didn't want to go home straight away so he popped over to mine for a bit.'

'Was he still with you at about half-past eleven, would you say?'

Amy nodded. 'Yeah, definitely.'

The police officer looked down at her notes. 'Okay. Do you have any idea why he might have phoned you around that time?'

Amy narrowed her eyes for a moment. 'Oh, he popped out to try and get some drink. For himself, I mean. If we touched my mum's stuff, she'd go mad.'

'Don't worry,' the officer said. 'You don't have to be eighteen to drink at home, and I'm not trying to catch you out on that. Do you know where Greg went to try and buy alcohol?'

Amy shook her head. 'I've no idea. He didn't find anywhere open, and he was only gone a few minutes. He called to say he couldn't be bothered to keep looking so was coming back.'

'And how long did Greg stay when he got back?'

'He stayed over.'

The police officer nodded slowly. 'How do you know Greg?'

Amy had been waiting for this question. 'He's my boyfriend's best friend.'

'Your boyfriend being…?'

'Lewis Hopkins.'

'And where was Lewis on the night of the fourteenth?'

'Uh, he'd been to the party with Greg, but he'd gone straight home afterwards. That's what Greg told me.'

'On his own?'

'Yeah, I presume so. I hope so.'

'But his best friend came over to yours and slept here overnight?'

Amy looked at her. 'Nothing like that happened, if that's what you're asking.'

'Not my place to ask, Amy. It just seemed a bit odd, that's all.'

Amy sighed. 'Lewis and Greg don't get on sometimes. Quite a lot, actually. They live together in the flat, but sometimes when they've had a couple of drinks they fall out. Lewis just sulks and sits by himself, but I get on really well with Greg.'

'What's Lewis like?' the officer asked.

Amy saw this as a chance to sow a few seeds.

'Uh, he's alright, I guess.'

'You guess?'

'Well, he gets a bit angry sometimes. You know what men can be like.'

'Angry how? Violent?'

Amy thought about this for a moment. 'I dunno. Not to me. Not really. But I've always wondered if he could. He just gets so angry about things, and ends up punching walls and stuff. I think that's why Greg has to get out of the flat sometimes, just to let him calm down.'

'How often do you see Lewis, Amy?'

Amy shrugged. 'Every few days or so. We're not joined at the hip or anything. I've not seen him for a few days. He's been acting a bit weird.'

'Weird? Weird how?'

'I dunno. Sort of evasive, I guess. Like something's wrong but he wouldn't tell me.'

The police officer nodded. 'Amy, would you be willing to testify this information in court, if required?'

Amy narrowed her eyes. 'Uh, yes. That'd be fine. Why? Why would anything be going to court? What's happened?'

The police officer looked at her and gave her a sympathetic smile.

45

It's odd knowing I'll only be in this cell for another few hours. Although I hate it here, I know it. Brian comes to me regularly and does what he can to comfort me. The police officers who work in the custody suite have been good to me, too. Not DI McKenna. She can go fuck herself.

I'm absolutely dreading the thought of going to the remand prison. At least here I'm on my own, not thrown in with other prisoners. I just can't bear the thought of having to be on a wing with murderers and violent criminals for the next three months. It'll finish me.

A large part of me just wants to end it all. Find the perfect opportunity to make a noose and kill myself. But then I'd have no way of ever proving my innocence. I'd go to the grave a criminal. Not only would I leave my boys without a mother, but they'd go through life believing their mum was a murderer who killed their grandad. The pain is excruciating.

After I told Brian about what happened with Lewis and Greg, he went off to try and track Greg down. Right now, he's my only hope. I have to pray that he knows where Lewis is, or that he knows someone who does.

I'm also hopeful that the police will find Lewis and speak to him. I just have to have faith that my account of what happened all those years ago was compelling enough for them to want to speak to Lewis about what happened to Roger.

I still don't see how it could be him, though. Or why. He killed a girl and went to prison for it. Justice was done. Surely after eighteen years he would have realised that and moved on with his life. Wouldn't he?

I didn't even testify in court against him. The only involvement I had was that my witness statement gave Greg an alibi and disproved Lewis's defence. But I believed Greg. I trusted him. I think I still do. I think.

And the thought that Lewis could have got into my house to steal and hide my mobile phone is just ludicrous. He would have needed a key to get in, and no-one has a key except me and Brendan. Even the boys don't have one. They never go out when we're not there, and in any case they'd only lose a key if we gave them one.

Setting up something like this would have required so much planning. I don't remember Lewis ever being like that. He was always a reactor, impetuous and knee-jerk.

If someone said something he didn't like, he'd hit them first and think later. I can't see him being the sort of person to plan something like this.

But what other options are there? I'm not the sort of person to create enemies. I barely even fall out with people. Not to the extent that they'd want to turn my entire life upside down, ruin my family, commit a murder and try to frame me for it.

The hatch on the door to my cell slides open and a police officer peers in. 'Do you want to come and make your phone call, Amy? We can give you ten minutes now.'

I look at him for a moment. 'What phone call?'

'Your solicitor gave us a phone number he'd found for you. Said it was a friend you wanted to call, but you didn't have the number to hand. If you can make it quick, you can do it now while we're quiet.'

I try not to smile. Good old Brian. Before I can get too pleased, though, the thought hits me that I'm about to speak to Greg. I haven't spoken to him in years, since about three months after what happened that day in court. What the hell am I meant to say? And there'll be police officers nearby, too, so I'll have to be careful with my words.

I can't miss this opportunity, though. God knows what effort Brian's gone to to track down Greg's number.

I follow the police officer down the corridor towards the custody desk. When we get there, he hands me a slip of paper with the number on and watches me dial.

The phone rings five or six times before it answers.

'Hello?'

I don't recognise the voice immediately. I'm not sure if I should. It's been a long time.

'Hi, is that Greg?'

'Yeah, speaking.'

'Greg, it's Amy Walker. Hennessy.'

There's silence at the other end for a few moments. 'You got married.'

'Yeah.'

'I thought you might. Blimey, I've not heard from you for years. What's up?'

'Nothing,' I say, before realising how ridiculous that is. 'Well, not quite nothing. I need to speak to you. I wanted to ask you something. About back then.'

'Alright,' Greg replies. I can tell he's not exactly relishing the prospect.

'Do you still speak to him?'

'No.' Greg answers firmly.

'Have you spoken to him? Or seen him?'

'No. People have seen him around, apparently, but he doesn't engage. He's not interested. Not that many people have exactly wanted to strike up conversation with him.'

'But you've not seen him yourself?'

'I moved away. I live on the south coast now. So no, I'm not likely to bump into him either. Not unless he fancies renting a holiday chalet off me. Which I very much doubt he does.' Greg's silent for a moment, and I can almost hear his thought process. 'What's up, Amy? Why now?'

I take a deep breath. 'I need to find him. I need you to help me find him.'

'No. Sorry, Amy. I've put all that behind me. I'm not getting involved. Whatever answers you need, I'm afraid I can't help you with them.'

'Wait,' I say, sensing that Greg might be about to hang up the phone. There's no way the police will let me make another call. 'Please. Just hear me out.' Greg doesn't say anything, but I can hear the faint hiss that tells me the line is still connected and he's still there. 'Something's happened. Recently. Something massive. I think he's done something. Something really bad.'

'Like what?' Greg asks, after a few seconds of silence.

I look over at the desk sergeant. He's not paying any attention to me, but he soon would if I answered Greg's question.

'I can't say. But I think he's... I think he's done it again.'

There's silence on the other end of the line.

'You think he's killed someone?'

'Yeah,' I say, looking over at the desk sergeant.

'Who?'

'My father-in-law.'

'Why would he do that?'

'Why do you think?'

The line goes quiet as Greg takes his time to digest this. His answer isn't what I'm expecting.

'Amy, I'm sorry to hear about your father-in-law but this really has nothing to do with me. I can't get involved. I just can't. Sorry.'

'No, wait. Greg. Please. He's set it up to make it look like I killed Roger. He's framing me, and he's not going to stop there. If he's done this to me, he'll do something to you too. Greg, I think he might try to kill you next.'

'I'm sorry, Amy.'

Greg puts the phone down and the call disconnects just as the desk sergeant rushes over and takes the phone from me.

46

SUNDAY 5 AUGUST, 7.20PM.

Brian spoke to the custody sergeant earlier and told him I had some new information I'd like to discuss. He told me they'd do a post-charge interview. I thought this would happen pretty quickly. After all, wouldn't they be keen to find out more information and ensure they've got the right person?

But no. It's only now, more than eight hours after I told Brian about Lewis — and four hours after speaking to Greg — that they've decided to call me through for the interview. I don't know if this is their way of trying to tell me they don't really care about what I have to say, or if they just want me to sweat it out and stay here as long as possible, but Brian tells me they're probably just short on staff.

We sit down around the table in the interview room and DI McKenna switches on the recording equipment.

'Amy Walker, I'm arresting you on suspicion of murder. You do not have to say anything, but it may harm your defence if you do not mention when questioned something which you later rely on in court. Anything you do say may be given in evidence. Do you understand all that?'

'We've already done all this,' I say. 'I was arrested at my front door yesterday morning.'

'Yes, but as we're now post-charge I'm required to caution you again under the Police and Criminal Evidence Act. Do you understand the caution I just gave you?'

I sigh. 'Yes. Yes, I do.'

'Good. Now, your lawyer, Mr Conway, tells us you have some new information which might be of benefit.'

I'm not sure who she thinks it might be of benefit to, or if Brian's given them any of the details, so I start with the basics.

'Yes. I think I know who might have killed Roger. I think I know who might have set it up to make it look like it was me who did it.'

'Okay,' McKenna says. 'Who's that?' Her tone of voice tells me nothing. It's straightforward, as if I've just called up a takeaway and she's taking my order.

'His name's Lewis Hopkins. He's an old boyfriend of mine.'

'You've been married a few years, haven't you?'

'Yes. He's from a long time ago.'

'How long?'

I swallow. 'Eighteen years.'

McKenna flashes a look to her colleague, then glances back at me. 'Why would a boyfriend from eighteen years ago — when you were, what, fifteen? — want to do something like this?'

I take a deep breath, then let it all out. 'Because I wronged him. I took someone's side against him and he got into trouble over it.'

'Why now?' McKenna asks. 'Why would he wait eighteen years?'

'Because he's been in prison.'

'I see. How long for?'

I shrug. 'I don't know. He got an eighteen year sentence, but I understand he probably got released years ago.'

'That's a long sentence. What was the charge?'

'Manslaughter.'

McKenna raises her eyebrows.

'I had nothing to do with it. Nothing at all. I was his girlfriend at the time. He went out to this stupid party with his friend, Greg. Apparently Lewis picked up a girl there and brought her back to the flat. Hannah Shaw, her name was. He... They... They had sex. Lewis and Hannah. She died. She was strangled. Lewis tried to blame Greg, but I told the police he came straight to mine from the party and was with me at the time Hannah died.'

'And was he?'

I look at Brian, who nods gently for me to continue. I swallow. 'No.'

'So you committed perjury.'

'My client was never called to give evidence in court, and at no point was she under oath,' Brian says.

'Alright. You perverted the course of justice, then.'

My emotions get the better of me, and I struggle to hold back the tears and the huge, sagging feeling in my chest.

'I didn't know what to do. Lewis was... He was horrible to me. And when I found out he'd gone home with this girl, I just... I mean, I totally believed he'd killed her. I didn't believe a word about him accusing Greg. Greg wouldn't have done anything like that. Greg was lovely. And I knew that if I didn't, Greg would be implicated in it and Lewis might get off. I did it for all the right reasons.'

'There's never a right reason to pervert the course of justice, Amy,' McKenna says.

'I know. I know.'

'This Greg. What's his surname?'

'Lawrence.' I try to gauge McKenna's thought process, but I can't. She doesn't seem particularly happy about it, though. Maybe she thinks I've tried to hoodwink her somehow.

'And you think Lewis held a grudge over this?' she says.

I look McKenna in the eye. 'He got sentenced to eighteen years in prison for manslaughter.'

McKenna leans back in her chair and crosses her arms. 'Yeah, you see, this is what I don't understand. That's a long sentence for manslaughter, especially seeing as you described it as more or less a kinky sex game gone wrong.'

I shake my head. 'I don't think it was that. He moved the body and hid it. He tried burying it in the woods. And he tried shifting the blame onto Greg. Even at the trial he wouldn't admit it. He pleaded not guilty the whole way along.'

McKenna nods slowly. 'None of that will have helped him much. But why would he come after you? And why would he do this, rather than just attack you? Why your father-in-law? And why not Greg?'

'I don't know. That's what I've been thinking about, but I can't make any sense out of it. The best I can come up with is that he thinks I should have stuck by him as his girlfriend. And me and Greg... Well, after the trial, we kind of got together. Not for long, but we did.'

'May I?' Brian says to me.

I nod. I don't know what he wants to say, but right now I just want a way out of this.

'My client told me she thinks Lewis's motivation behind doing this could have something to do with the fact that he feels he spent years of his life behind bars for a murder he didn't commit. She told me that perhaps that was his motivation for ensuring she did the same. It's almost a direct form of revenge, if you will.'

I look at Brian, trying not to show any emotion on my face. I didn't say anything of the sort. He glances back at me, a look on his face that says *Trust me, roll with this.* He must have misconstrued my shocked stare. All that's going through my mind is the processing of that thought. That maybe Lewis didn't kill Hannah Shaw. That perhaps...

'And do you have any evidence of this?' McKenna asks.

'Of course not,' Brian answers. 'You had my client in custody within an hour or two of the crime being committed. The first she'd heard that her father-in-law had died was in the back of a police car. She's been in one of your cells ever since.'

McKenna nods slowly. 'And why didn't you tell us any of this in your police interviews, Amy?'

I blink rapidly. 'I don't know. I didn't think. I was just shocked and stunned. I was trying to work it all out in my head. You were asking me all these things about phones and cars and CCTV and none of it made any sense. My brain was just an absolute mess.'

'We feel,' Brian says, trying to regain some calm, 'that Greg could be in some considerable danger. Lewis would also have a cross to bear with his old friend, and there's a distinct possibility that his life could be in danger.'

McKenna takes a deep breath. 'I understand what you're saying, but that's more or less just a wild guess, isn't it? Is there any evidence or anything at all — other than a random stab in the dark — that might suggest that?'

I talk before Brian can. 'Please. You have to arrest Lewis. Speak to him. Find out where he was. See if he's got an alibi. Check his phone records, I dunno. Just look into it. Please. I can't handle another minute in here. I didn't do anything!'

'Amy, we can't just go around arresting people because you've thrown us a random name of someone you pissed off eighteen years ago.'

Brian gets there before me. 'Detective Inspector, I think we need to look at the options here. If you're right, and this has nothing to do with Lewis Hopkins, then what's been lost? An hour or two speaking to him. If you're wrong and we're right, and Lewis gets to Greg first, you'll have blood on your hands.'

'With respect, Mr Conway, that doesn't answer my question. That's not evidence.'

'Gathering evidence is your job, inspector, not mine. I strongly advise you to speak with Lewis Hopkins.'

'And strongly advising me is my boss's job, Mr Conway, not yours.'

'Speak to Greg, then,' I say. 'Just speak to Greg. He might... I don't know. Just please. Do something.' I look at Brian and nod. He hands a slip of paper across the desk to McKenna.

'This is his telephone number. Please, inspector, don't let one missing phone call end a man's life.'

47

The sun seemed to be shining brighter than ever before as they left the court and walked down the steps towards the street.

The trial had attracted hardly any media attention, having opened on the morning of the 9/11 attacks and closed a couple of days later while the news was still filled with images from New York.

The prosecution had seen Greg and Amy as their key witnesses. Amy, fortunately, hadn't needed to speak in court. Her witness statement had been enough on its own, together with the DNA evidence found in the boot of Lewis's car and the semen found in the body of Hannah Shaw.

The defence had dropped the shifting of blame onto Greg shortly before the trial began, presumably because they knew they were onto a hiding to nothing. The police told Amy and Greg that it was a ploy by the defence to try and get Lewis the shortest possible sentence. If he tried shifting the blame or lying in court, his sentence would only be harsher.

Amy knew Lewis would hate that. He couldn't stand thinking he'd been wronged, and she could see the pure hatred in his eyes as she sat in the courtroom. He barely took his eyes off Amy and Greg the whole time.

Lewis had shown very little remorse in court. The fact he'd been under the influence of alcohol and drugs when he killed Hannah Shaw, plus the removal and concealment of her body, led the judge to hand him an eighteen-year sentence.

For Amy, it felt like a huge weight had been lifted from her shoulders. Justice had been done.

Ever since finding out what had happened that night, she'd wondered how at risk she'd been. From what she understood, or had worked out, Hannah didn't want to have sex with Lewis, or had asked him to stop, but he'd carried on. Amy could easily see how he would have done this. He'd done the same with her many times before. Fortunately, she hadn't struggled. Hannah had, and it had resulted in her death.

And although he hadn't testified as such in court, Lewis had maintained to the bitter end that it had been Greg who'd killed Hannah. Amy would never forgive Lewis for that. Not only had he raped and killed an innocent girl, but he had tried to shift the blame onto his best friend, the guy who'd been nothing but supportive to Amy. He'd been her rock.

She'd wondered whether, after the trial was over, her and Greg might get together. He'd never actually said anything about that — he wouldn't — but she would be lying if she said the thought hadn't crossed her mind. There would be plenty of time. Now, she just wanted to get her life back to normal and forget all about Lewis Hopkins.

48

People who say prison is easy are talking shit. I've only been here a few hours but I'm just about ready to give up.

The magistrates' court was a formality. A waste of time, almost. I was barely in the building five minutes, before I was brought here.

The remand prison is a specialist women's prison. Almost everyone here is waiting for their trial. I wonder how many are innocent, but judging by those I've seen it doesn't look like many.

If I felt alone in custody at the police station, this is something else entirely. This feels like proper prison. It is proper prison.

The staff have tried to be nice to me, but it's mostly just formal. I guess they need to try to keep people on side, but still showing that there are rules and regulations that need to be adhered to. The vast majority of people are in here because they can't keep to rules, after all. But I feel like I'm being treated like a naughty schoolgirl. I've done nothing wrong.

At some point in the afternoon — I've now lost track of time — I'm told it's visiting time. I tell the prison officer this means nothing to me. My husband and kids are unlikely to be visiting me any time soon, and I'm not interested in seeing anybody else. But he's insistent. Someone is here to see me.

I still have no idea who my visitor is as I walk to the visiting room and am guided through the double doors that lead to the large open area of tables and chairs.

But the moment I walk in and see that face, I recognise it immediately.

'Greg.'

'Hi,' Greg replies, forcing a smile.

'You said you didn't want to speak to me.'

I don't know what to feel. I feel confused, angry, hurt. But hopeful at the same time. Why is he here, less than twenty four hours after that phone call?

I sit down, on the other side of the table from him. The prison officers sit around the edges of the room, watching, but too far away to hear any of the conversations.

'How have you been?' Greg asks.

'Oh yeah, fine. Having a whale of a time. You really should try it sometime. Far better than Butlins. Cheaper, too.'

Greg wisely ignores my sarcasm. 'I've been thinking about what you said,' he says. 'About Lewis. I didn't really want to say anything on the phone earlier, but an old friend of mine reckons he saw Lewis coming out of a shop in town a week or so ago.'

This hits me like a thunderbolt. I'd been under the impression Lewis had moved away, like Greg did.

'In town?' I ask.

'Yeah.'

'Which friend?'

'Someone I used to know. He messaged me on Facebook. He said he recognised Lewis straight away, and remembered the story from the news all those years ago. He remembered I was friends with him back then and got in touch to find out what had happened since.'

I sit in stunned silence for a few moments. Lewis is here. In town.

'You said on the phone he'd been seen, but you never said it was so recent.'

'I know.'

'Why didn't you tell me this on the phone?' I say. 'That he was seen so recently, so close to where I live?

Greg shrugs. 'I dunno. I just didn't think it was relevant.'

'You didn't think it was relevant? I specifically called you for the first time in eighteen years and asked you if you or anyone you knew had seen Lewis, and you didn't think it was relevant that the answer was yes?' Another thought crosses my mind as I say this. 'Hang on. You said you live on the south coast. You rent out beach huts.'

Greg swallows. 'Yeah. I do.'

'We're a long way from the south coast.'

Greg looks around, as if the walls are going to offer some sort of explanation. 'I drove up here. I thought it'd be better to talk face to face.'

'Why? Why not just answer my questions on the phone? Why not just call the police and tell them what you knew?'

'Because…' He trails off, clearly not wanting to finish his sentence.

'Why, Greg?'

Greg sighs. 'It was what you said at the end. About me being next.'

I stare at him, unable to comprehend what I'm hearing. 'So you were perfectly fine when I phoned you to tell you I thought he'd murdered my father-in-law and set me up to look like the killer. That wasn't a problem for you. But the moment I said you might be next, all of a sudden it becomes a huge priority.'

'It's not like that.'

'It very fucking much looks like that to me,' I say, pushing my voice through gritted teeth, trying not to look too angry. I really don't want the prison officers coming over now. 'You haven't changed a bit, have you? You've shown your true colours once again. It's all about self-preservation for you. You don't give a shit about anyone else but yourself.'

'Amy, I understand this is a stressful time for you, but don't you want to hear what I've got to say? Don't you want to know where he is?'

When he tells me he understands it's a stressful time, I want to bite his head off. Instead, I just look at him, the expression on my face perfectly clear.

I stand up, and indicate to the nearest prison guard that I'm ready to leave. 'No. I don't. If you're really that bothered, call the police.'

49

MONDAY 6 AUGUST, 6.15PM.

When the call had come in to say that Greg Lawrence had made contact with the police and had some information about Lewis Hopkins and Amy Walker, McKenna quickly decided she would visit him herself.

She had a good eye for a bullshitter, she felt, and needed to judge for herself whether or not there was any truth in what Amy had said about Hopkins.

He'd told the call handler he was staying at a small hotel on the edge of town. McKenna knew the one. She'd been there before. It was laid out more like an American motel than anything she'd ever seen in England before. The rooms were more like chalets, arranged in a court-yard fashion around the small carpark. It looked more like the Bates Motel from *Psycho* than your typical Premier Inn or Travelodge.

That thought wasn't far from her mind as she turned

off her car's engine and scanned the doors for number seven. *Lucky number seven*, she thought to herself, although she had to admit there was very little that was lucky or fortuitous about her visit this evening.

She spotted room seven and pointed it out to her colleague, DC Mark Brennan, before the pair walked over towards it and McKenna knocked on the door.

She waited a few seconds before calling out, 'Mr Lawrence? It's Detective Inspector Jane McKenna. You asked to see us.'

'Maybe he's giving us the runaround,' Brennan suggested, shoving his hands into his trouser pockets.

'Why ask us to come and see him then? He's not local. He's up here for a reason.' She knocked on the door again. 'Mr Lawrence? Can you open the door please?'

Brennan sighed and rocked on his feet, his hands still shoved deep into his trouser pockets. 'Think we're wasting our time here.'

McKenna ignored him and tried the door handle. To her surprise, the door yielded and opened.

It creaked on his hinges as it swung backwards, and it took a moment for the police officers' eyes to adjust to the relative darkness inside.

When their eyes had adjusted, though, Brennan spotted the remains of a broken drinks glass on the floor.

'Skip,' he said, pointing towards it. He needed no more words. The implication of what this meant was clear to both of them.

McKenna switched on the light and took a closer look around the room, before looking down at her feet. From the back of the room near the rear window, all the way to the front door of the hotel room, were two faint but jagged black lines, occasionally stopping before starting again, marked onto the laminate flooring.

She bent down and rubbed at one with her fingernail. 'Rubber. Probably off the heel of a pair of shoes.'

'Like someone being dragged across the floor you mean?' Brennan asked.

McKenna nodded. 'That's exactly what I mean. You stay here.'

She jogged across the car park and into the reception area. A young girl was seated behind the desk, texting on her mobile phone.

McKenna waited a full two seconds, then cleared her throat as loudly as she could.

'Oh, sorry,' the girl said. 'World of me own. Are you checking in?'

'No. Well, sort of. I'm checking in on one of your guests. Mr Gregory Lawrence. In room seven. Have you seen him?'

The girl looked in the vague direction of room seven, then shook her head. 'Don't think so. But I only came on shift about ten, fifteen minutes ago.'

McKenna sighed. 'I don't suppose there's any use me asking if you saw anyone going into or leaving room seven? Or a car being here for a short period of time?'

'Sorry. Like I said, I've only been here fifteen minutes or so.'

And haven't looked up from your phone since, McKenna wanted to say.

'And who was on before you?'

'Michael. He just left a few minutes back.'

'Do you have contact details for him?'

'Yeah, got his mobile number if you want that.'

McKenna thought for a moment. 'Actually, let's go one better. Can you call him and ask him to come back here? We need to ask if he saw anything suspicious while he was on shift.'

The girl looked worried, and narrowed her eyes. 'Erm, yeah, okay,' she said. 'Why, what's happened?'

McKenna pursed her lips and glanced around the room. 'That's what I need to find out.'

50

Shortly after speaking to Michael, the previous recep-
tionist who'd just clocked off shift at the hotel, McKenna
put the call out to trace Lewis Hopkins's home address
and potential whereabouts.

It had taken a while for anything to come back, but
McKenna had mentioned Hopkins's previous convictions,
which should have made him a little more traceable.

Finally, though, the call came.

'We've got an address for him,' the officer on the
other end of the phone said, reeling off an address
around twenty miles away. Far enough to not bump into
people from his old life on a regular basis, but close
enough to keep in the loop if he needed to. 'It took a bit
of time, though. Turns out he changed his name by deed
poll not long after leaving prison. Maybe he wanted to
start afresh.'

By moving barely twenty miles away? McKenna thought.

'This is the weird thing, though,' the officer added. 'He works in town. He's gone to the effort of changing his name so he can have a new life, but he's still working in the same town where he was living eighteen years ago. Strange or what?'

Not in the slightest, McKenna thought. 'That's good stuff. Thanks. Tell me, out of interest, where does he work?'

McKenna recognised the familiar sound of someone desperately looking for information on a computer screen.

'Uh… he's an accountant, by the looks of things,' the officer said.

McKenna's face dropped at the same time her heart rate started to increase. 'Okay. Where?' She listened to the sound of fingers tapping on a keyboard, a couple of moments of silence and then the response came.

'A company called Morris & Co. Do you know it?'

McKenna took a deep breath and tried to compute her thoughts, desperate to work out what this all meant. All she knew is it wasn't good. 'Yeah, it's come up once or twice. And what's his name now? What did he change it to?'

'Well, this is what made me think he just wanted to start afresh and stay anonymous, see. If I wanted to change my name because I was bored of it, I'd pick something cool like Tony Funk. Or Blaze Maguire. Wouldn't you?'

McKenna really didn't want the conversation to be going off on a tangent now. 'I don't know,' she said. 'I've never really thought about it. I just want to know what Lewis Hopkins's name is now.'

'Boring old Simon Robinson, apparently. Worse than his old name if you ask me. So I think my theory still holds water.'

McKenna made a noncommittal noise. Although her colleague's theory might hold water, she was quickly starting to realise that hers didn't.

51

PCs Michelle Jackson and Joshua Ross pulled up at the address they'd been given — a small cottage in a village they didn't have cause to visit very often. It wasn't the sort of place that was crawling with crime. In fact, there wasn't very much going on here at all, at any point.

All they knew is that they were looking for a man called Simon Robinson, who had formerly been known as Lewis Hopkins, who'd already served a conviction for manslaughter and was to be arrested for murder if they could find him.

They had clearance to force entry to the property if necessary, particularly if they suspected he was inside or there was some sort of danger. The number of people who thought the police had to have a warrant to enter a premises with force was a common source of amusement. It was up there with 'I don't want to press charges' and suggesting that traffic cops should be out catching murderers and sex offenders.

'Car's here. Should be someone in,' Joshua said.

Michelle knocked on the front door of the cottage, and began peering through the front windows. Joshua — Rylan to his friends, owing to his visual likeness to a former reality show contestant — made his way round the back of the property, through the unlocked side gate and pushed at the back door. It was locked, but the door wouldn't hold much force. He decided to test it.

It only took one fairly mild shoulder-barge and the door was open. 'Mr Robinson?' Joshua called, but got no reply.

By now, Michelle had joined him round at the back of the house, just in time to find Joshua rummaging through the under-stairs cupboard, which had been left slightly ajar. On the floor inside was a carrier bag, containing a blonde wig, woman's bra and what looked like a pair of chicken fillets.

'Bit weird, this,' Joshua said.

'Mmmm. Not the worst I've found. I'll call it in.'

While Michelle was speaking to DI McKenna to let her know the address was empty apart from a bag full of some very weird shit, Joshua noticed a car key hidden in the folds at the bottom of the bag.

'Not where I'd keep my car keys,' he said to Michelle, walking past her and making his way back round to the front of the cottage.

Sure enough, it unlocked the blue Ford that was sitting on the driveway. There was nothing inside the car of any interest — it was almost immaculate — so Joshua opened the boot to take a look inside. The boot was empty, apart from a pair of car number plates.

He took them out and pulled the car boot down, to take a look at the registration of the car itself.

'Michelle, take a look at this,' he called to his colleague, who had come to see what he was playing at.

'Yeah, we've got a pair of registration plates in the boot of his car, ma'am,' Michelle said.

The response on the other end of the phone was a moment of deafening silence. 'What's the registration number on them?' DI McKenna asked.

'Totally different to the one on the car. The ones in the boot are Foxtrot Oscar One Seven Uniform Tango Alfa.'

Michelle could almost hear the rush of breath leaving McKenna's lips.

'Jesus Christ. Thanks. That's fantastic. And you're sure there's no-one in the house?'

'Pretty sure.'

'Right. Stay at the scene. I'll send backup.'

Michelle had no idea how some fake tits and a pair of number plates could be so significant, but she was certainly looking forward to finding out.

52

Jane McKenna didn't have time to feel guilty or nervous about what the fallout would be regarding Amy Walker. Right now, her sole focus was on finding Lewis Hopkins and Greg Lawrence.

At times, it was painfully slow trying to extract information from third party organisations, but when life was in immediate danger it was extraordinary how quickly people would turn over.

It had taken barely an hour for Lewis's bank to provide details of recent transactions on his account — held in the name of Simon Robinson. He'd paid a deposit to a hire car company two days earlier, on the Saturday afternoon.

This baffled McKenna. Lewis had a car at his home address. She thought perhaps he didn't want to use the Fiesta as it was too similar to Amy's car. Indeed, if her theory was correct, that had been the whole purpose in him buying the Fiesta.

But why hire a car using his own debit card? Was he really cocksure enough to think no-one would link it to what happened all those years ago, simply because he'd filled in a form to change his name? Did he not think the two names were linked on systems somewhere? If it was McKenna, she would have used cash. But then again the hire car company would have done a lot of extra checks and likely put additional security measures in place. It would have aroused suspicion.

Besides which, he had to be pretty confident the police wouldn't be looking into him at this stage. And he was almost right. He'd set it up perfectly. McKenna didn't know how, but she was starting to get an idea. It didn't matter if he was caught by someone tracing the car after he'd got to Greg, because by then he'd have done what he needed to do. He just needed to get to both of them before the police worked it out and apprehended him. What came after was irrelevant. Unless he'd planned that, too. Unless…

'Fuck,' she said, out loud, attracting the attention of one of her colleagues in the major incident room.

'What is it?' her colleague asked. 'Something wrong?'

McKenna shook her head. 'No. Not at all. In fact, something's very very right. For him, anyway. It's beautiful. Poetic. It all makes perfect sense.'

'Sorry, boss. Not with you.'

'Right,' McKenna called, making sure her voice was heard right across the office. 'Everyone stop what you're doing and listen up.'

A few officers, who were on phone calls, simply cupped the receiver to continue the call they were on.

'Absolute number one priority right now needs to be on finding Lewis Hopkins — alias Simon Robinson — and Greg Lawrence,' McKenna said. 'Think about it for a moment. Hopkins was wronged by Amy and Greg all those years ago. In his mind, he served a sentence for a crime he didn't commit. Maybe he didn't. But he did the time, and as far as he's concerned it was because of them. Even if he didn't kill Hannah Shaw back then, I firmly believe he did kill Roger Walker. Let's get into his mind for a minute. He's already served the sentence. That's what you get in exchange for killing someone, right? Now let's assume he didn't kill Hannah. He was in credit. He was owed a murder. And if one of Amy or Greg goes down for that murder, equilibrium is restored. The other one… Well, they're owed their own special sort of come-uppance too, aren't they?'

'Like what?' an officer asked.

'I don't know yet. He could be trying to kill Greg. But that would mean two murders and only one sentence, so perhaps he's happy to get caught for that one. This, for him, is all about justice. It's all about fairness and equilibrium. Or maybe he doesn't want to get caught. Maybe he's done his time. In which case, there's only one way out as far as he's concerned. Kill Greg, then kill himself.'

McKenna could see from the faces looking her way that the penny had dropped. Not only was there an apparent kidnap situation, but they were hunting a murderer who could well kill again and ultimately evade capture forever.

'So we need to start looking pretty damn quickly,' McKenna said. 'As for *where* we start looking... I think I know who might have the answer to that.'

53

I feel a surge of hope in my chest as the prison officer tells me to follow her. It's not visiting time, it's not a scheduled work or exercise session. I know — I've memorised them all. There's been very little else to do. That means this is something different, something outside of what's expected. I silently pray there's been a breakthrough and Brian's efforts to expose the truth haven't gone unnoticed.

I'm taken across the landing, down the stairs and through a door, which leads into another corridor and, ultimately, a small side room.

It reminds me of the rooms you see in American prison dramas, where one person sits one side of a plate of perspex and the visitor sits on the other, speaking only through phones. This is a bit different: there are no phones. It looks more like a post office or bank counter, except we've both got chairs.

Sitting on the other side is Detective Inspector McKenna.

'Amy. This was the quickest way to see you, without having to go through all the security checks,' she says, before I even sit down, not pausing for breath. 'Some new evidence has come to light. I won't go into details, but our sole focus right now is finding Lewis Hopkins and Greg Lawrence. Lewis has a new name now. Did you know that?'

I narrow my eyebrows. 'No. No, I didn't.'

'I didn't think so,' McKenna says. 'He changed it when he left prison. His name now is Simon Robinson.' She looks at me for a moment, watching as the realisation sets in. I know that name. 'Yes,' she says. 'That one.'

'But… but it can't be him. I would have known.'

'How many times have you met Simon?'

I think back. 'Well, none. Everything was done remotely. He dealt with our accounts, but as part of the firm. It was a team effort. It was usually David who came in, if anyone did.'

'Did you ever speak to Simon on the phone?'

It takes me a moment to realise the answer. 'No. Only email.'

The realisation hits me like a ten tonne truck. In all the time I've been discussing accounts and bookkeeping queries with Simon Robinson, it was Lewis all along. Why? How? I start to hyperventilate, panicking at how long this has been planned for. Has he been watching me that long? Sneering, knowing I didn't know his true iden-tity? How long has this been going on?

'Amy, you need to help us. We think this was all planned long in advance. It's been symbolic for him. We think it's still symbolic. Is there anywhere you can think of where Lewis might have taken Greg?'

It's only then that I realise what's happened. 'Taken him? What do you mean taken him?'

'I don't have time for the detail, Amy. We went to meet with Greg and he wasn't there. There were signs of a struggle. Simon's house was a treasure trove of evidence. We've got him bang to rights, but we need to find him. And Greg. Before something else happens.'

I've never been good at thinking under pressure. I know I desperately need to think and help McKenna but all I can hear is the roaring in my ears and the blinding lights in front of my eyes. All I can think of is everything I've been through, everything this woman has put me through, and how desperately I've wanted it all to be over. How Lewis has been watching me, living inside my life for so long, without me even noticing. I've been an island, separate from reality for longer than I ever realised, and now I'm being thrust right into the middle of it all, told that I've got the key, got the answer.

But I haven't.

'I… I dunno,' I stutter. 'I don't know what you want me to say.'

'Is there anywhere you can think of that he might

have taken Greg? Somewhere that has some sort of symbolism for them both. Something from back then? Something connected with the crime, maybe.'

I shake my head. 'Not connected with the crime. That's not his style. That's too… crude. Lewis is a nasty piece of work, but he's clever. There'll be something deeper than that.'

'Like what?'

'I'm trying to think,' I say, holding back the tears as I desperately rack my brains for the answer. I know there's something here. Somewhere. Something mentioned long ago, something I wondered about and which…

'Denton Lakes,' I say.

McKenna nods at her colleague, who quickly leaves the room, reaching for his mobile phone. 'Why there, Amy?'

'I don't know. There was some sort of connection. They went there when they were kids. And something else. I never quite worked out what, but I got the feeling something happened there.'

McKenna looks at me, and I see her Adam's apple bob in her throat as she swallows. 'Okay. Sit tight, alright? We'll keep you posted on what happens.' She stands and turns to leave, before stopping and turning back to me. There's the slightest glint of tears in her eyes. 'And Amy? I'm sorry.'

54

They'd been at Denton Lakes for over an hour, sitting on the sandy bank, the sun slowly disappearing over the canopy of the trees as the heat of the day became a dull orange glow that skipped across the water.

Simon had said all he'd needed to say. He'd spent so long being Simon, speaking as Simon, he was surprised at how easy it was to become Lewis again. Perhaps some things never went away.

It had been easy for him to change his name and become someone new. He'd lost his true identity years earlier anyway, so this was simply another adjustment that needed making.

'You have no idea what it's like, do you?' he said to Greg, who was bound at the wrists and ankles with cable ties, plastic tape across his mouth stopping him from shouting out. There was no-one here anyway, but Simon wasn't about to take the risk. This had always been a very secluded spot. In a way, it was that seclusion that had started this whole chain of events, and it was the seclusion that would end them.

'I'll tell you what it's like,' he continued, 'spending your whole life watching out for someone. Carrying a secret like that and trying to protect them. And why? So you could stick two fingers up to it and fuck me over when the spotlight finally lands on you.'

Greg looked at him, his eyes emotionless.

'I presume you recognise the spot,' Simon said. 'Just over there, I think it was. You know, I dream about it every night. Always have. I can see her face smiling at me, her long green dress fluttering in the breeze as she walks over. If I close my eyes hard enough I reckon I could count the polka dots. It's like the image is burned on the insides of my eyelids. I can see the trees, the branches moving, hear the leaves rustling and the water lapping gently over the rocks. And then it changes. Everything else around it goes dark. There's silence, until the sound of her head exploding as the log hits it. I don't even hear her hit the ground. I just hear the sound of my own breathing and see you standing over her, your chest heaving. And why? Because she told you off for pissing around and called you a useless little twerp. Sad thing is, she was right. She knew she was right, and she knew I knew she was right. That's why she smiled at me. That's why that was the last thing she did.'

Simon looks over at the water, sees the light dancing on the surface, the movement of the trees reflected in its glass surface.

'They arrested three people, you know. Released them all, too. I don't know if I ever told you that. We always tried to forget it and put it behind us. Something like that is fucking huge when you're an adult, but it's crippling when you're nine. Who'd have guessed there were three known blokes locally who matched the description we gave the police? I can still remember it now. About this much taller than your mum,' he says, holding his hands six inches apart, 'black jacket and trousers, white trainers. Ran off in that direction.' Simon points towards the car park. 'It's the only time I've been thankful for rain, although I didn't know it at the time. If it hadn't started pissing down ten minutes later, they'd have expected to find footprints. But then, who's going to doubt two nine-year-old boys? Who's going to think one of them's just bashed his own mum to death and managed to keep a straight face?'

Simon sighed and shook his head, letting out a small laugh. 'Funny thing is, if I'd just told them what happened, that would have stopped everything. The whole chain of events. I wouldn't have had to keep that secret. Wouldn't have had to keep watching you, wondering when the next time would be. Wouldn't have had to devote my entire fucking life to protecting you and your secret, just because I had the bad fortune to grow up with you, almost like brothers. Like blood brothers, remember? Our mums went to see that show. Told us about it. Joked it could have been us. So we did it. We cut our palms and held hands. And spent the next month making sure our parents didn't see that hand. It worked. It made us think it was real.

'And that's why I didn't tell them. Because I thought it *was* real. I thought that bond went further than anything else. And I thought that right up until the moment I found out you'd fucked me over. Right up until Hannah Shaw. Right up until you told the police you weren't there, told them you didn't crush her windpipe, told them she wasn't your second victim. And then you had the temerity to drag Amy into it, to convince her to give you an alibi, to pinch her from under my nose and drag her into bed while I was rotting in jail. Do you still wonder why you're here?'

Greg's face showed no emotion. He shook his head slowly. There was no wondering to be done. There never had been.

JANE MCKENNA DUG her fingernails into the palms of her hands as the cars rolled silently into the car park at Denton Lakes. Her express instruction had been no sirens, no blue lights. The last thing they wanted was to spook Robinson.

She'd had the tactical firearms unit on standby ever since they'd discovered he and Greg were missing. She had no way of knowing if Robinson was armed, but by now she knew he was almost certainly an experienced killer, and most likely had the intention of killing Greg. And he wouldn't be planning on doing that empty handed.

Air surveillance would have made things much easier, especially with the use of infrared cameras to find heat sources in the area of the lakes, but the regional heli-copter would have been too noisy — and expensive — and using a drone would have been impossible because of the level of tree cover.

Fortunately for them, though, a call had come in for McKenna on the journey to Denton Lakes from one of her DCs. They'd been doing some digging into the two men's pasts and discovered that Greg Lawrence's mum had been murdered at Denton Woods when the boys were nine years old. It hadn't taken them long to scour the files and find an aerial map of the area, on which the murder location had been marked. McKenna didn't know why, but she was sure this was where they'd gone.

With everyone clear on where they were headed, the team began to move forward in silence.

SIMON KNEW he'd said all he could possibly say, yet he

felt he wanted to say a whole lot more. He'd had years thinking about this, planning it, and he'd felt sure he knew every single word. But when it came to it he'd just opened up and spilled everything at once, the words tripping over themselves to get out of his mouth.

He didn't know what good it would do. He knew Greg would never feel any sort of remorse. Sure, he could put on a great act of being sympathetic or caring, but Simon knew it was all an act — a carefully choreographed routine he'd learned by watching people who actually had emotions.

The silence was beautiful. It was all beautiful, in its own way. Everything had come full circle, and it felt right.

That was until the silence was broken by the sound of a twig breaking underfoot, somewhere off in the distance. Simon's ears had become attuned to the silence, to the natural sounds here, and the distant snapping of a twig might as well have been a neutron bomb.

Greg heard it too. He could tell from the glint in his eyes and the corners of his mouth desperately trying to pull free of the tape and twist up into that shit-eating grin he thankfully hadn't seen for years.

Without a second thought, he dipped his hand into his rucksack and pulled out the knife. It was a hunting knife — a gorgeous, hand-made one he'd bought from a shop in the Scottish Highlands a couple of years back. He'd known then what its purpose would be, which deranged beast would die at its cut. But until then it had been a treasured possession, a symbol that promised him his time would come.

And that time was now.

ONE OF THE firearms officers at the front of the group raised his arm in the air and slowed to a stop. The others stopped too.

'Armed police! Put the weapon down!' the firearms officers yelled, stepping forward in unison and spreading out to multiply their angles on Robinson. 'Put down the weapon or we will shoot!'

'Put the knife down, Simon,' McKenna said. The weapon was already at Greg's throat. She knew the firearms officers wouldn't be able to do anything to stop him killing Greg. One flick of the wrist and it would be done. Even if they shot him now, the reflexive action and jolt of his body would likely decapitate Greg. 'We know what you've been through, Simon. We know who you are. We can talk about it, we can make sure justice is done.'

'It already has been done,' Simon shouted back, tears stinging his eyes. 'This is just the final closure.'

McKenna didn't give up. She never gave up. She knew that even if Simon did end this by cutting Greg's throat, there'd be a volley of bullets hitting him within half a second. They wouldn't shoot to kill — there would be no point, especially as they knew in this situation

Simon's next move would likely be to turn the knife on himself. Here, they'd aim to injure and disable, preventing him from taking his own life. 'This doesn't need to happen, Simon. If you put the knife down, we can listen to you and find out the truth. Don't give him the easy way out.'

Simon let out a noise that sounded like a laugh. 'This is nothing to do with him. This is me ridding the world of a monster. I'm doing you a favour. And I'm ending the story here.'

Before McKenna could open her mouth, Simon pulled the knife across Greg's throat and began to stab at the side of his neck, before the first bullet made contact and sent him reeling onto the floor.

I remember when I was a kid, when the six-week summer holiday felt like it lasted for years. This past week feels very much the same.

There's been an odd but comforting return to normality, as much as we can ever get back to where we were. Things will always be different, but for now it's reassuring that everyone is at least making the effort.

The police had no trouble extracting the truth from Lewis. As far as he was concerned, his story was complete other than for one small detail, which I feel sure he'll rectify at some later date. Until then, I'll always be waiting for the call that tells me he hanged himself in his prison cell or slit his wrists with razor blades.

And when that call comes, how will I feel? I'm pretty sure I'll feel nothing, much the same as I do now. All that matters to me is that I'm back with my family, scarred and bruised as we are, but somehow still stronger than ever.

McKenna had felt the need to tell me every detail of what Lewis had done, how he'd gained his accountancy qualification in prison and got a job working for Morris & Co specifically because he knew he'd be able to get closer to me. She told me how he'd doctored false invoices and made it look like I'd been embezzling money from the company.

Everything had been planned with the most incredible detail. He'd been in our house months back, having a meeting with Brendan while I was away. He knew I was away. I recall him asking when Brendan and I were free, and specifically saying the only day he could do was when I was away. He'd struck gold when Brendan mentioned us leaving our phones to charge in the kitchen overnight, and had spotted the spare key sitting openly on the shelf. He'd pocketed it, had a copy made and then returned to our house in the dead of night and replaced the original. It had been easy, he told the police. And that's why he'd felt so comfortable coming back last week to take my phone and put his plan into action.

I didn't know whether to be shocked or impressed when the police told me this. I couldn't be surprised as I always knew how clever Lewis could be. The only thing that shocked me was Greg. To discover that he'd killed his own mother at the age of nine and got away with it had turned my blood cold. He'd been so calm and convincing that night eighteen years ago, when he'd murdered Hannah Shaw only minutes earlier and wanted me to help frame his best friend, the friend who'd kept his secret for so many years. His blood brother.

Part of me can see why Lewis reacted the way he did. The deception and double-crossing must have seemed momentous. As far as he was concerned, I was in league with Greg and everyone was against him. And he stewed on that in prison for years.

Do I forgive Lewis? No. But I'm sure my stance will soften with time. Things are too raw right now to really feel anything.

The organisational machine is already in full flow, trying to organise Roger's funeral. The kids are, of course, distraught that their grandad's dead. Fortunately, Brendan never told them why I disappeared shortly after. He said someone had made their grandad die and Mummy was helping the police to catch the person. I wonder if Harry maybe twigged something, but he didn't let on. One day I'll tell them both. I think this family has had enough of secrets for now.

The policy apology came swiftly. I was taken into a meeting with the Chief Constable, who personally apologised to me for what had happened. She said there was a process I could follow in order to get justice for myself, but that for now we should let the air clear and decide how we move forward from here. That was fine with me. All I wanted was to see my husband and my kids.

Brendan's been fantastic. He's devastated by what's happened, of course, but he's been doing his best to try and make family life normal again. They're out at football again this morning. He got the boys up bright and early and made them breakfast, before getting their kit together. Just like any normal Saturday morning.

It's going to be another beautiful day. I've barely seen the sun, and if I have I haven't noticed it. Today's the first day I feel the warmth. I bring the mug of tea to my mouth and drink the last couple of mouthfuls, before putting my book down on the table and heading back inside for a refill.

Just as I switch the kettle on, the doorbell rings.

I swallow, instinctively, my hands shaking a little as I steel myself and tell myself not to be so silly.

I make my way to the front door, take a deep breath and open it.

It's Jane McKenna.

'Amy,' she says. 'I won't take up too much of your time. I just wanted to drop by and say how truly sorry I am for what you've been through. I take full responsibility. I… I thought you should have this,' she says, pulling some folded sheets of paper from her inside suit jacket pocket. I take them from her. 'It's a form for the IPCC, the Independent Police Complaints Commission. Once you've managed to get your head round everything, you should fill it in and detail how you were treated.'

'What will happen?' I ask her.

She shrugs. 'I've no idea.'

'Will you be reprimanded?'

'Probably,' she says. 'But please don't let that change anything. You've a right to some sort of retribution here. Like I said, I really am so sorry.'

I nod, and look back at the paper in my hands.

I lift it up in front of my face and tear it in two.

GET MORE OF MY BOOKS FREE!

Thank you for reading *The Perfect Lie*. I hope it was as much fun for you as it was for me writing it.

To say thank you, I'd like to invite you to my exclusive *VIP Club*, and give you some of my books and short stories for FREE. All members of my VIP Club have access to FREE, exclusive books and short stories which aren't available anywhere else.

You'll also get access to all of my new releases at a bargain-basement price before they're available anywhere else. Joining is absolutely FREE and you can leave at any time, no questions asked. To join the club, head to adamcroft.net/vip-club **and two free books will be sent to you straight away!**

If you enjoyed the book, please do leave a review on

the site you bought it from. Reviews mean an awful lot to writers and they help us to find new readers more than almost anything else. It would be very much appreciated.

I love hearing from my readers, too, so please do feel free to get in touch with me. You can contact me via my website, on Twitter @adamcroft and you can 'like' my Facebook page at facebook.com/adamcroftbooks.

For more information, visit my website: adamcroft.net

IN HER IMAGE

Alice Jefferson has a new friend. He wants her dead.

He's been in her house while she's been sleeping. He follows her every time she leaves the house. She knows exactly who he is.

The police can find no trace of him having ever existed.

And then she uncovers a shocking secret that turns her entire world upside down, and leaves her unable to trust anybody — even herself.

Click here to buy it now.

HER LAST TOMORROW

Could you murder your wife to save your daughter?

On the surface, Nick Connor's life is seemingly perfect: a quiet life with his beautiful family and everything he could ever want. But soon his murky past will collide with his idyllic life and threaten the very people he loves the most in the world.

When his five-year-old daughter, Ellie, is kidnapped, Nick's life is thrown into a tailspin. In exchange for his daughter's safe return, Nick will have to do the unthinkable: **he must murder his wife**.

With his family's lives hanging in the balance, what will

Nick do? Can he and his family survive when the evil that taunts them stems from the sins of his past?

Click here to buy it now.

TELL ME I'M WRONG

What if you discovered your husband was a serial killer?

Megan Miller is an ordinary woman with a young family — until a shocking discovery shatters her perfect world.

When two young boys are brutally murdered in their tight-knit village community, Megan slowly begins to realise the signs all point to the lovable local primary school teacher — **her husband**.

But when she begins to delve deeper into her husband's secret life, she makes discoveries that will make her question everything she knows — and make her fear for her young daughter's life.

Facing an impossible decision, she is desperate to uncover the truth. But once you know something, it can't be unknown. And the more she learns, the more she wishes she never knew anything at all...

Click here to buy it now.

ACKNOWLEDGMENTS

Before I was an author, I used to read these bits at the back of books and wonder how much help the named people actually provided.

Now I know.

Although 'Adam Croft' may be plastered across the front of the book, the truth is there are a number of people who provided invaluable help and support in getting this book finished.

My wife, Joanne, is always my first reader and makes sure all the REALLY daft mistakes get sorted out before anyone sees the book.

The biggest thanks for this book, though (sorry Jo) must go to Graham Bartlett, ex Detective Chief Superintendent and Commander of Brighton & Hove Police, whose assistance has been invaluable. He's the reason Peter James's books are so authentic and true to life, and I was keen that this book be as realistic as possible. Without Graham, that wouldn't have happened.

Thanks also go to Sacha Black for her unique brand of support, to Stuart Bache for yet another incredible book cover and to Lucy Hayward for her eagle eye.

To Annabel Merullo, Jonathan Sissons, Laura McNeill and all the film & TV people at Peters, Fraser & Dunlop — your enthusiasm for my work and my career is much appreciated. Thank you for being so keen on me for two and a half years — I'm pretty sure that's more than my wife managed.

And the hugest thanks of all must go to every member of my VIP Club — all 40,000 of you — for your support and encouragement every day. You're what makes it all worthwhile.

ABOUT THE AUTHOR

With more than **a million books sold to date**, Adam Croft is one of the most successful independently published authors in the world, and **one of the biggest selling authors** of the past year.

Following his 2015 worldwide bestseller *Her Last Tomorrow*, his psychological thrillers were bought by Thomas & Mercer, an imprint of Amazon Publishing. Prior to the Amazon deal, *Her Last Tomorrow* sold more than 150,000 copies across all platforms and became **one of the bestselling books of the year**, reaching the **top 10** in the overall Amazon Kindle chart and peaking at number 12 in the combined paperback fiction and non-fiction chart.

His *Knight & Culverhouse* crime thriller series has sold more than 250,000 copies worldwide, with his *Kempston Hardwick* mystery books being adapted as audio plays starring **some of the biggest names in British TV**.

In 2016, the *Knight & Culverhouse Box Set* reached storewide **number 1 in Canada**, knocking J.K. Rowling's *Harry Potter and the Cursed Child* off the top spot only weeks after *Her Last Tomorrow* was also number 1 in Canada. The new edition of *Her Last Tomorrow* also reached storewide **number 1 in Australia** over Christmas 2016.

During the summer of 2016, two of Adam's books hit the ***USA Today*** **bestseller** list only weeks apart, making them two of the most-purchased books in the United States over the summer.

In February 2017, *Only The Truth* became a worldwide bestseller, reaching **storewide number 1** at both Amazon US and Amazon UK, making it the **best-selling book in the world** at that moment in time. The same day, Amazon's overall Author Rankings placed Adam as the **mostly widely read author in the world**, with J.K. Rowling in second place.

Adam has been featured on BBC television, *BBC Radio 4*, *BBC Radio 5 Live*, the *BBC World Service*, *The Guardian*, *The Huffington Post*, *The Bookseller* and a number of other news and media outlets.

In March 2018, Adam was conferred as an Honorary Doctor of Arts, the highest academic qualification in the UK, by the University of Bedfordshire in recognition of his achievements.

Adam presents the regular crime fiction podcast ***Part-***

ners in Crime with fellow bestselling author Robert Daws.